Buford P. Sez

Buford P. Sez

Al Staggs

RESOURCE *Publications* · Eugene, Oregon

Resource Publications
A division of Wipf and Stock Publishers
199 W 8th Ave, Suite 3
Eugene, OR 97401

Buford P. Sez
By Staggs, Al
Copyright © 2013 by Staggs, Al All rights reserved.
Softcover ISBN-13: 978-1-7252-9427-1
eBook ISBN-13: 978-1-7252-9429-5
Publication date 12/2/2020
Previously published by The Intermundia Press, LLC, 2013

Table of Contents

Preface

Friends and Family

This and That

Health and Such

Religion and Politics

Bufordpedia

Preface

Buford P. is a composite of men I encountered every day when I was growing up in the rural town of McAlmont, Arkansas, population 1,900. The Bufords of McAlmont were mostly small farmers, railroad men, truck drivers, and carpenters who had truly earned their education in the school of hard knocks. Many of them had fought in World War II or the Korean War and thus understood firsthand the cost of their freedom.

They spent their lives working hard, raising families and enjoying the great outdoors. Regardless of their lack of formal education, they possessed an abundance of common sense and knew instinctively how to live courageously and abundantly without regard to worldly riches or recognition. They didn't have any patience with pretense or pomposity and they didn't have the time or the inclination to read great books. But they had an uncanny knack for getting right to the core of matters. I was often surprised by their keen insight, and I was always captivated by their wonderful sense of humor.

This book is dedicated to the Bufords of McAlmont.

Friends 'n' Family

Love does mean never havin' to say you're sorry. It's knowin' that the one you love already knows it and loves you back in spite of it.

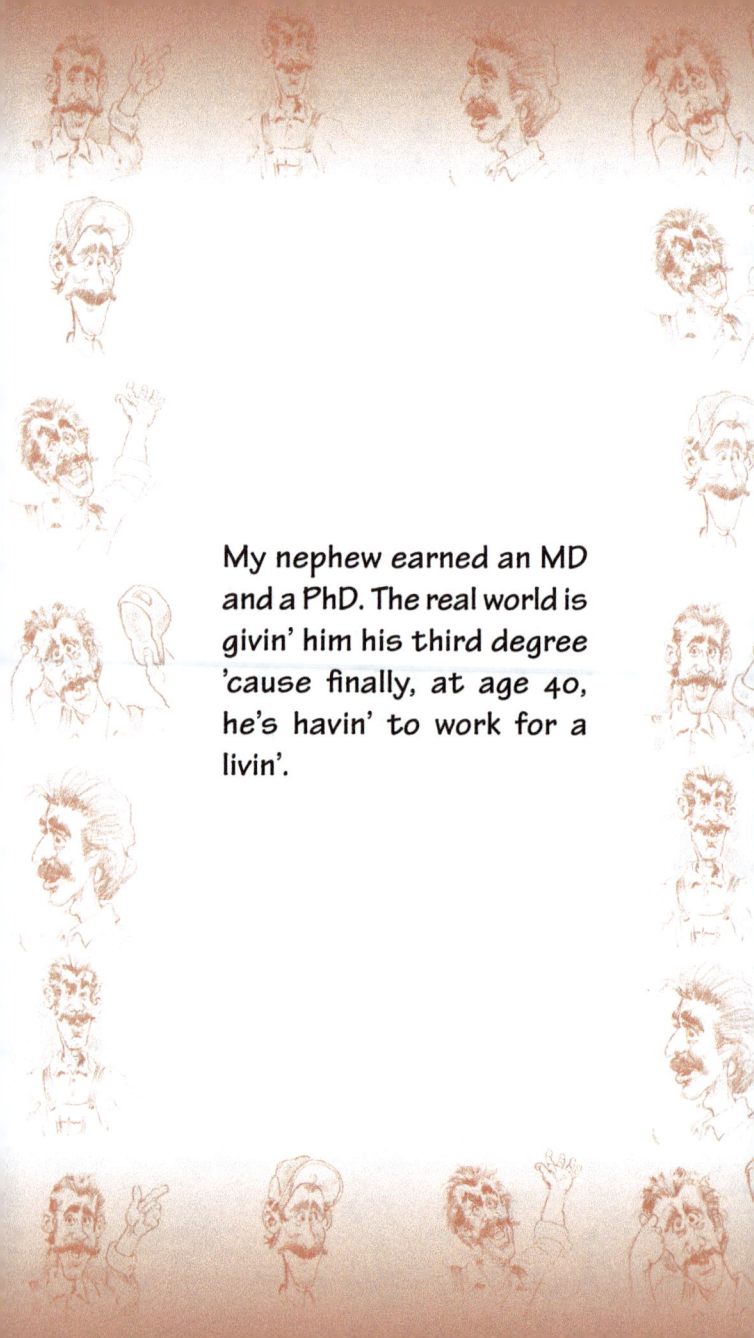

My nephew earned an MD and a PhD. The real world is givin' him his third degree 'cause finally, at age 40, he's havin' to work for a livin'.

I'm leavin' my kids something they'll remember me by — my debts.

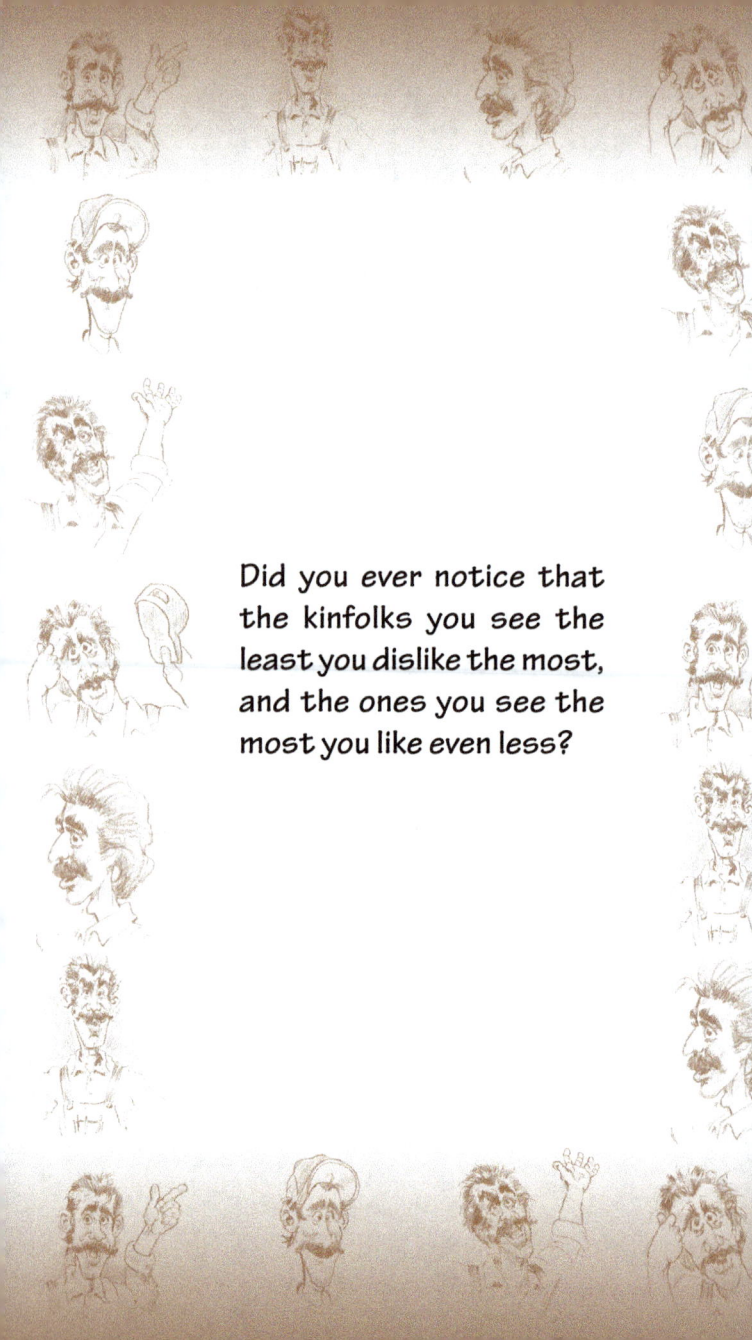

Did you ever notice that the kinfolks you see the least you dislike the most, and the ones you see the most you like even less?

After my brother-in-law had a string of affairs, my sister accidentally damaged the brakes on his sports car. He was 43. She said that she stayed true to their vow 'til death do us part.

I wouldn't be caught dead with another woman. What fun would that be?

I've gotta hand it to my mother-in-law. She's never said a single negative word to my face. Of course, she's never let me set foot in her house so she only saw my face at the wedding.

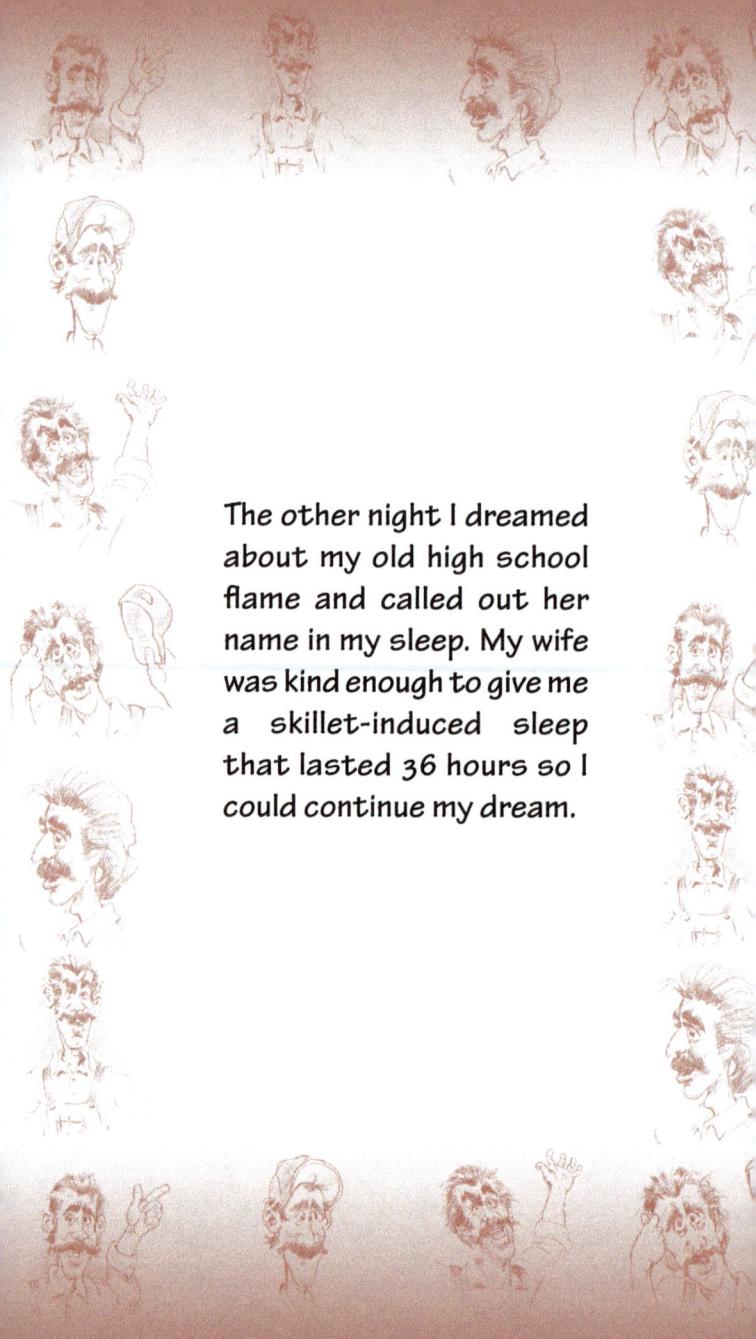

The other night I dreamed about my old high school flame and called out her name in my sleep. My wife was kind enough to give me a skillet-induced sleep that lasted 36 hours so I could continue my dream.

My wife said that seein' our kids grown makes her feel old, but it was raisin' 'em that made me feel old.

I pray for my kids every day. I pray that I can forgive 'em for all the meanness they did to me when they were little.

I have a word of encouragement for parents whose kids are goin' through a period of rebellion: don't worry, folks, your kids'll get over it by the time they have children of their own.

My advice to couples thinkin' about startin' a family is to continue just thinkin' about it.

When I was 16, I got a speedin' ticket while I was staying with my aunt and uncle. They told me they were ashamed that I was their nephew. I told 'em I felt the same way.

My kids never caused me a minute of sleeplessness. Actually, it'd have to be measured in months and years.

I was leanin' back in my chair on the front porch the other day when my wife walked up to me and asked what in the world I was doin'. I told her I was lookin' up at the sky and thinkin' about the wonders of the heavens. She said I'd be right up there with 'em if I didn't get off my tail and do some work.

My wife has tried about every diet there is with little success. In fact, it wasn't until I took up cookin' that dietin' worked for her.

It's downright impossible to bring up youngsters these days. By the time you're smart enough to raise 'em right and have enough money to put clothes on their backs, you're too darned old and tired to care.

My oldest boy came back from his first year in college claimin' that he already knew it all. I told him it was a good time to quit then 'cause that sure would save me a bunch of money.

When my wife and I first married, she claimed that I was the greatest man alive. The other day she told me that for the past 42 years I've been doing my best to prove her wrong.

My neighbor has a doctor's degree in English. I suppose that's why he talks to me so much—he's tryin' to cure my English.

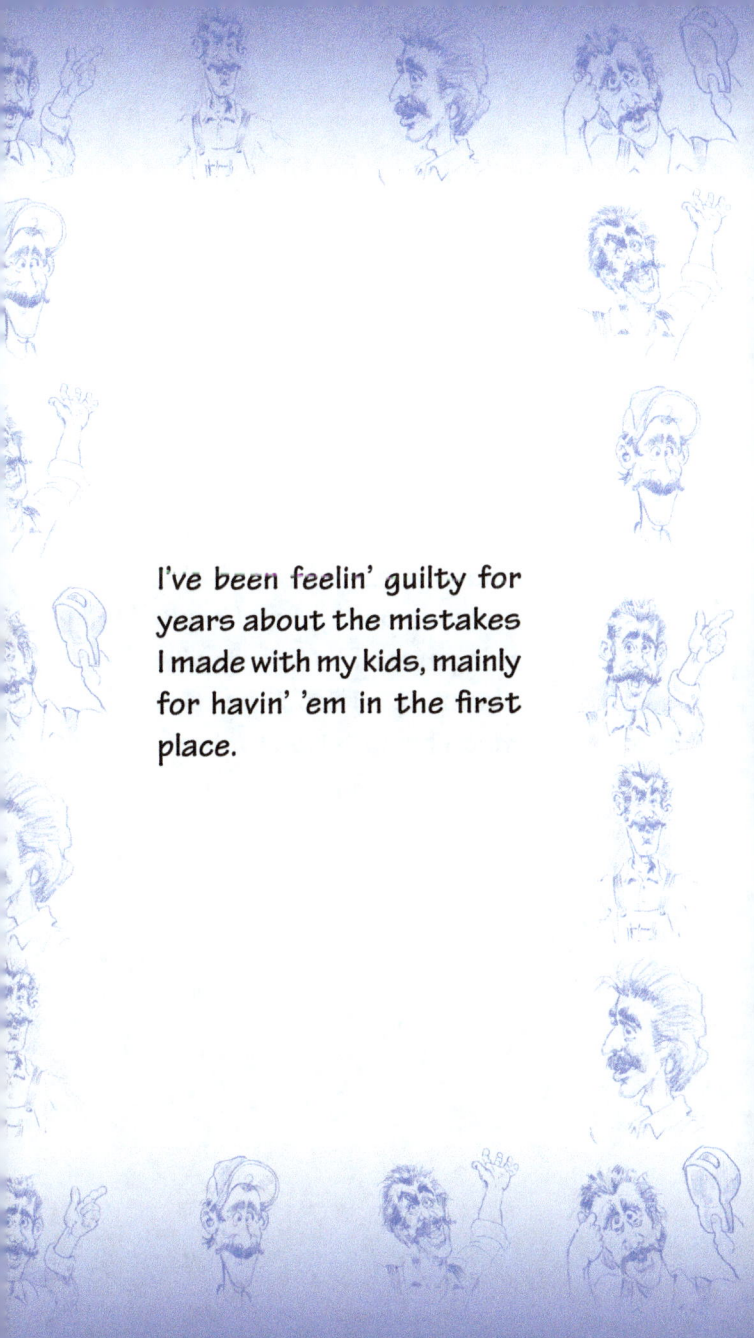

I've been feelin' guilty for years about the mistakes I made with my kids, mainly for havin' 'em in the first place.

I have a $250,000 life in-
surance policy, but I can't
bring myself to tell my wife
about it. That'd be too
much temptation for her.

I told my wife that when I die I want to be cremated. She asked me, *You gotta match?*

The secret to our long marriage is that for 40-plus years we've both been lookin' high and low for that secret and haven't found it yet.

My kids remind me that bad behavior is hereditary. Their mama's nature just slips out ever so often.

If you asked me if I've been happily married for all these years, I'd have to say yes. If I said no, there'd be a new widow in town.

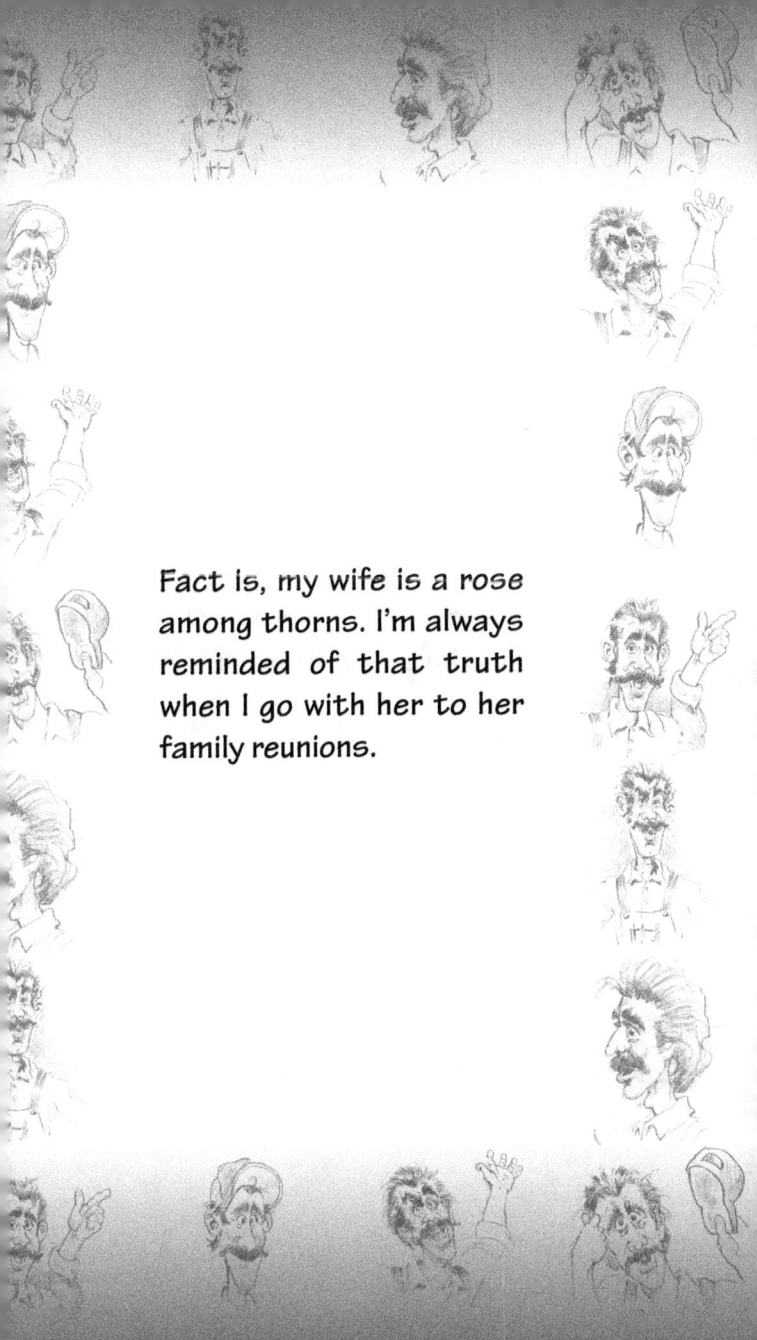

Fact is, my wife is a rose among thorns. I'm always reminded of that truth when I go with her to her family reunions.

There's no such thing as empty nest syndrome. Our kids have grown up and left and it's empty nest bliss at our house.

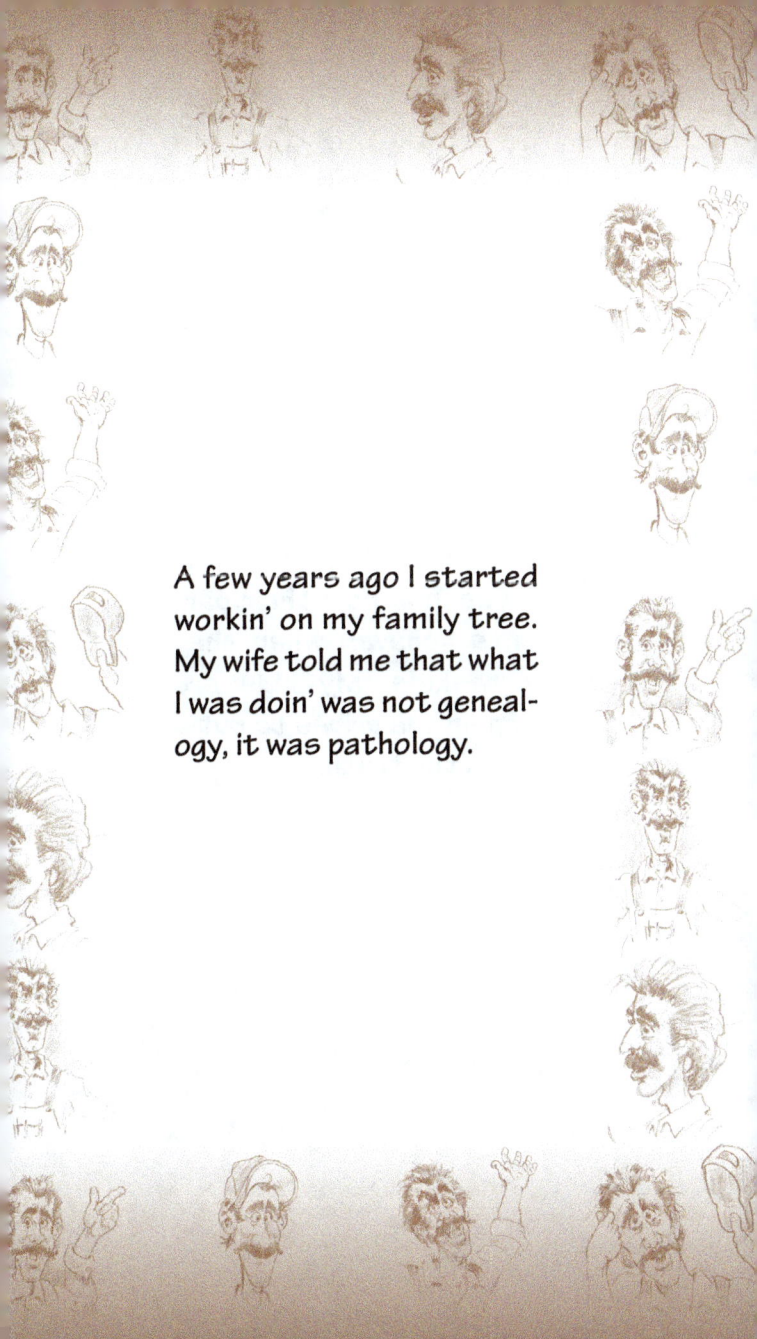

A few years ago I started workin' on my family tree. My wife told me that what I was doin' was not genealogy, it was pathology.

My grandkids are startin' to ask me how their parents behaved when they were kids. My kids are sendin' me bribes to put a lid on the truth.

When my dad drank heavily, he always said it was because of tryin' to feed us seven kids. Boy, did we kids have a lot of power over our dad.

My wife told me that if I don't straighten up she'll have me committed. I told her that I'm already committed—to her, and look what that's done to me.

My neighbor said he's goin' to start a truck garden next summer. I asked him what he would use for fertilizer in a truck garden—motor oil?

One of our kids went off to college and studied psychology and began to blame me and his mama for all of his problems. When he started havin' kids of his own, me and his mama became saints and experts.

I gave up gamblin' after my first marriage.

I was born during the Great Depression. My father was depressed 'cause he already had six boys to feed, and my mother was depressed 'cause she wanted a girl.

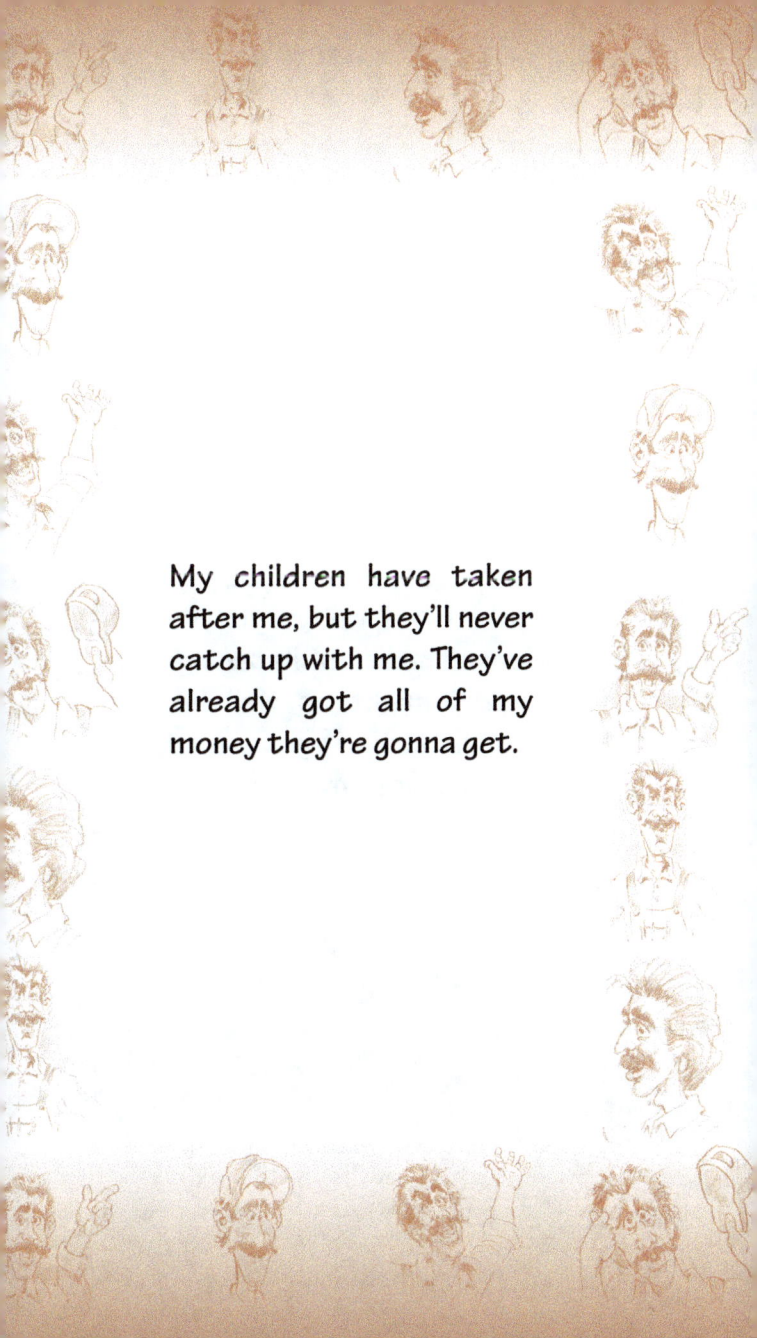

My children have taken after me, but they'll never catch up with me. They've already got all of my money they're gonna get.

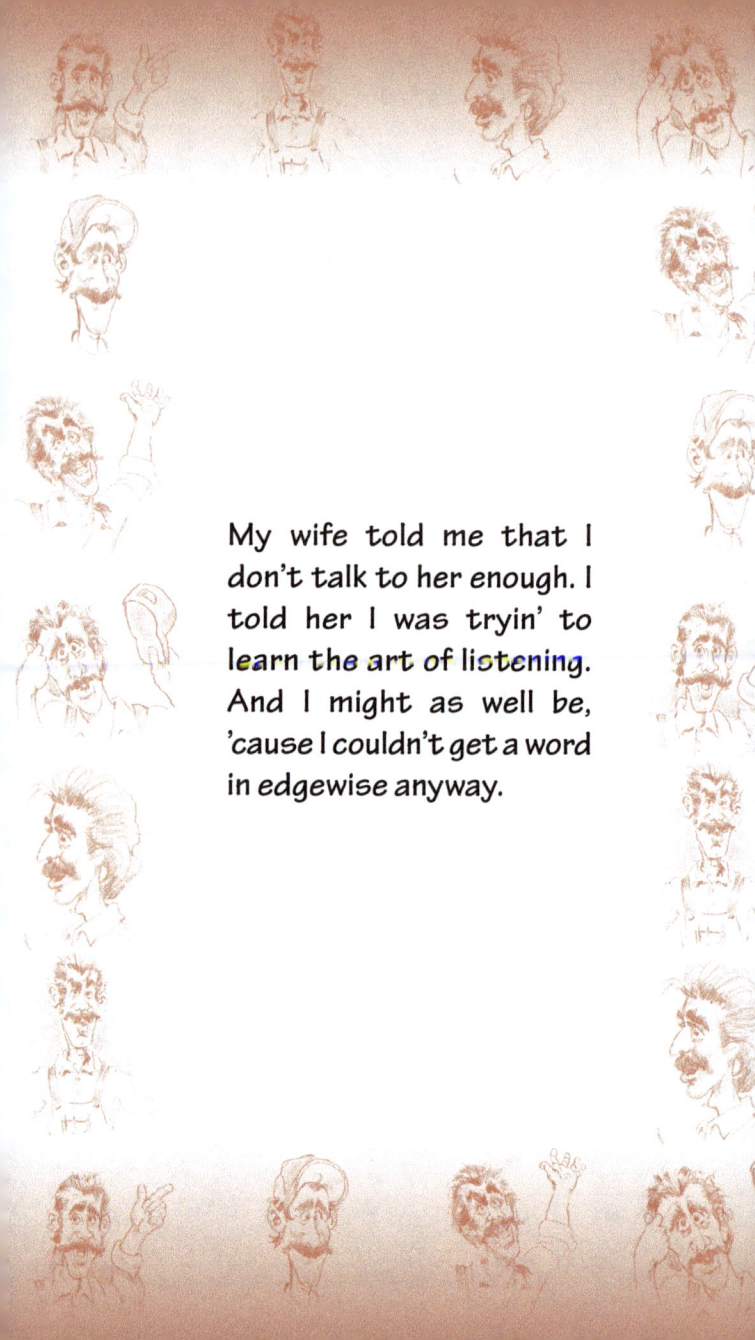

My wife told me that I don't talk to her enough. I told her I was tryin' to learn the art of listening. And I might as well be, 'cause I couldn't get a word in edgewise anyway.

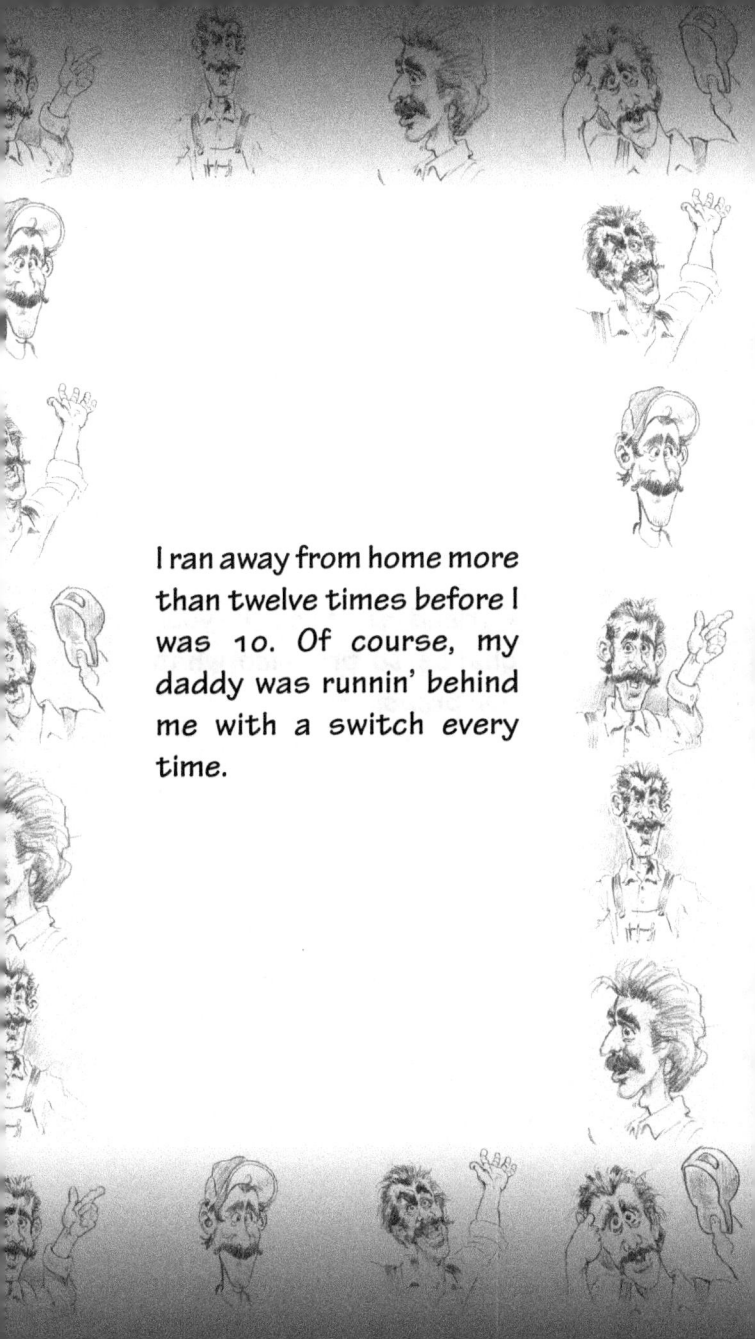

I ran away from home more than twelve times before I was 10. Of course, my daddy was runnin' behind me with a switch every time.

A friend in need can be your chance to practice what you preach.

I'm never gonna ask my wife if she's ever regretted marryin' me. Sometimes it's just best to believe what you want to believe.

Sure, I've looked at other women in my life. But after learnin' what it takes to make a relationship work, just a look will do.

I have a neighbor who brags that he's never taken a single drink in his life. Judgin' from the way he staggers out to the mailbox most mornings, it seems to me it would have been good if he had just taken a single drink.

My daddy was a fount of wisdom. He would tell me such things as, *Son, don't never eat on an empty stomach.*

My first girlfriend in high school wrote in my annual, *Buford, don't ever change.* I haven't. I'm as ignorant now as I was then.

Children usually mirror the best and the worst in us.

My wife is as sweet a person as you'll ever find, but I know not to get on the wrong side of her. That would be at the sharp end of a butcher knife.

My wife put a sign in our kitchen that says, *Don't give the cook any beef.*

Parents who neglect to discipline their children also do a great disservice to their future grandchildren.

My wife told me the other day that I was the man of century — the 19th century.

When I was born, I was supposed to grow up to be a cowboy, except my parents ran out of genes.

After bein' kept awake for five straight nights by my neighbor's dog, I can say for sure that I know a mutt whose bark is *much* worse than his bite.

This 'n' That

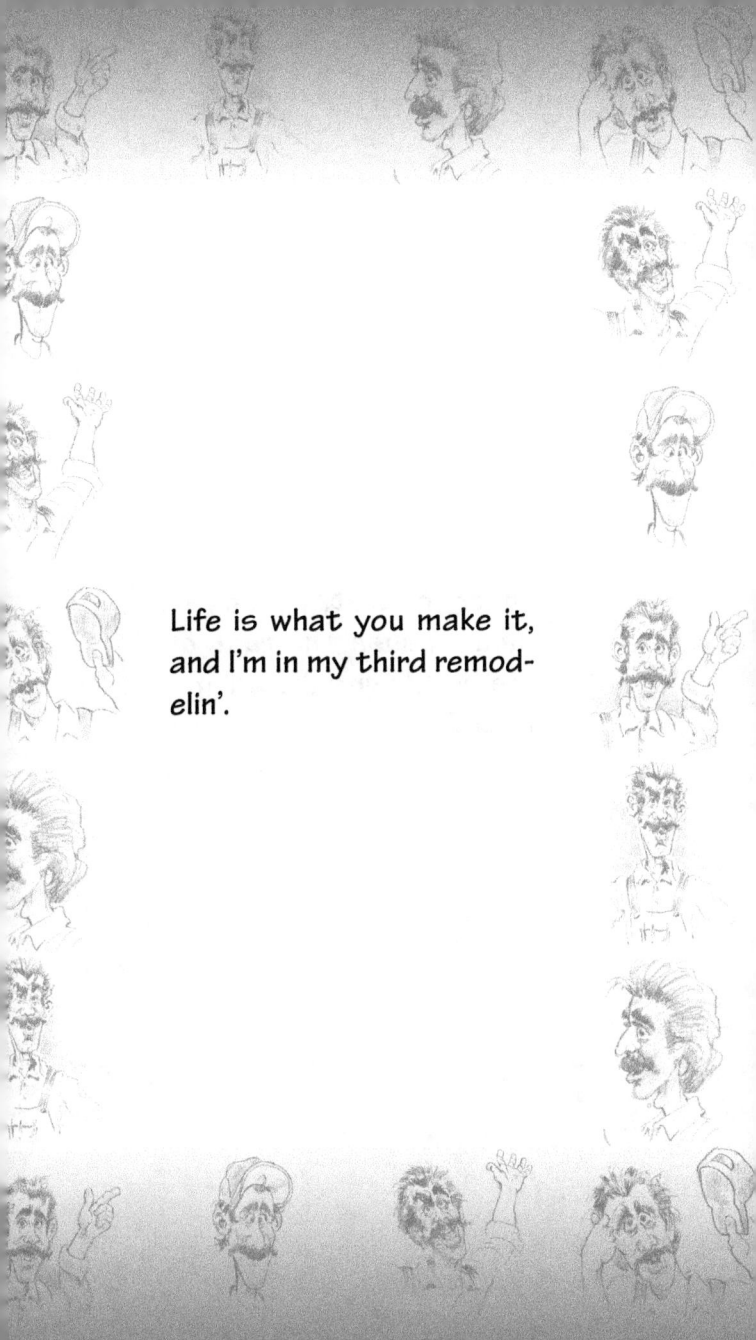

Life is what you make it, and I'm in my third remodelin'.

I'm tryin' to stay young at heart 'cause the rest of me is downright dilapidated.

It's not when a couple are newlyweds that love is blind. It's when a couple has been married fifty years or so and their hearts can still skip a beat when they look at each other.

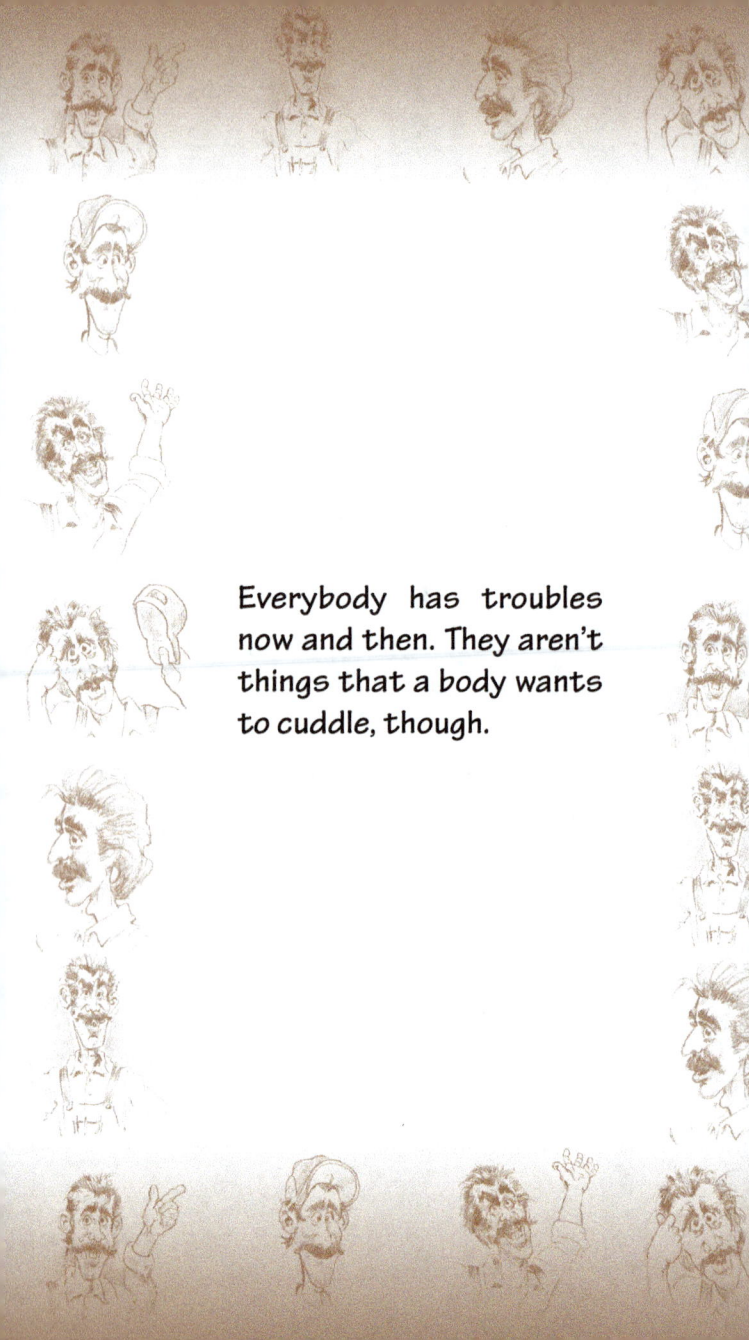

Everybody has troubles now and then. They aren't things that a body wants to cuddle, though.

When I was in high school, I came within an inch of winnin' the state championship in the mile run — that is, within an inch and four hundred yards.

My problems go back to childhood. I was born poor and haven't got over it yet.

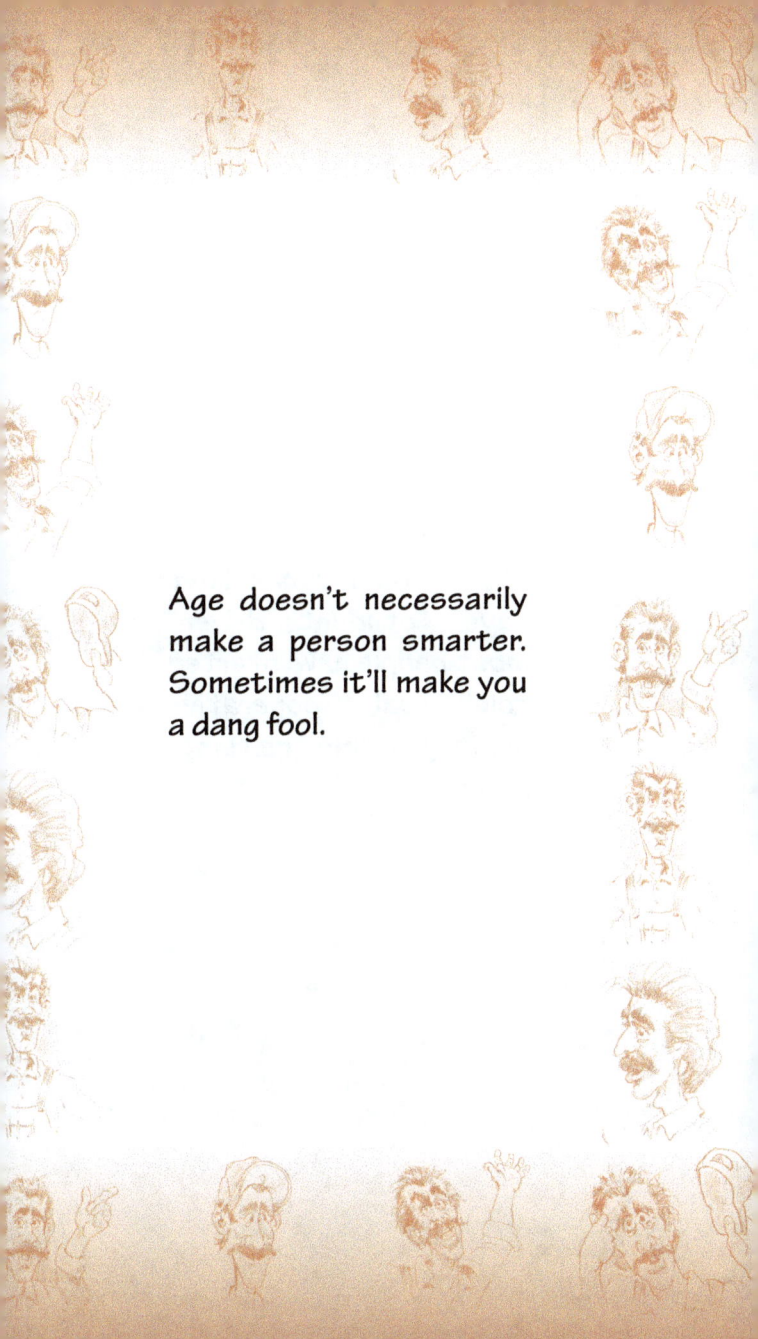

Age doesn't necessarily make a person smarter. Sometimes it'll make you a dang fool.

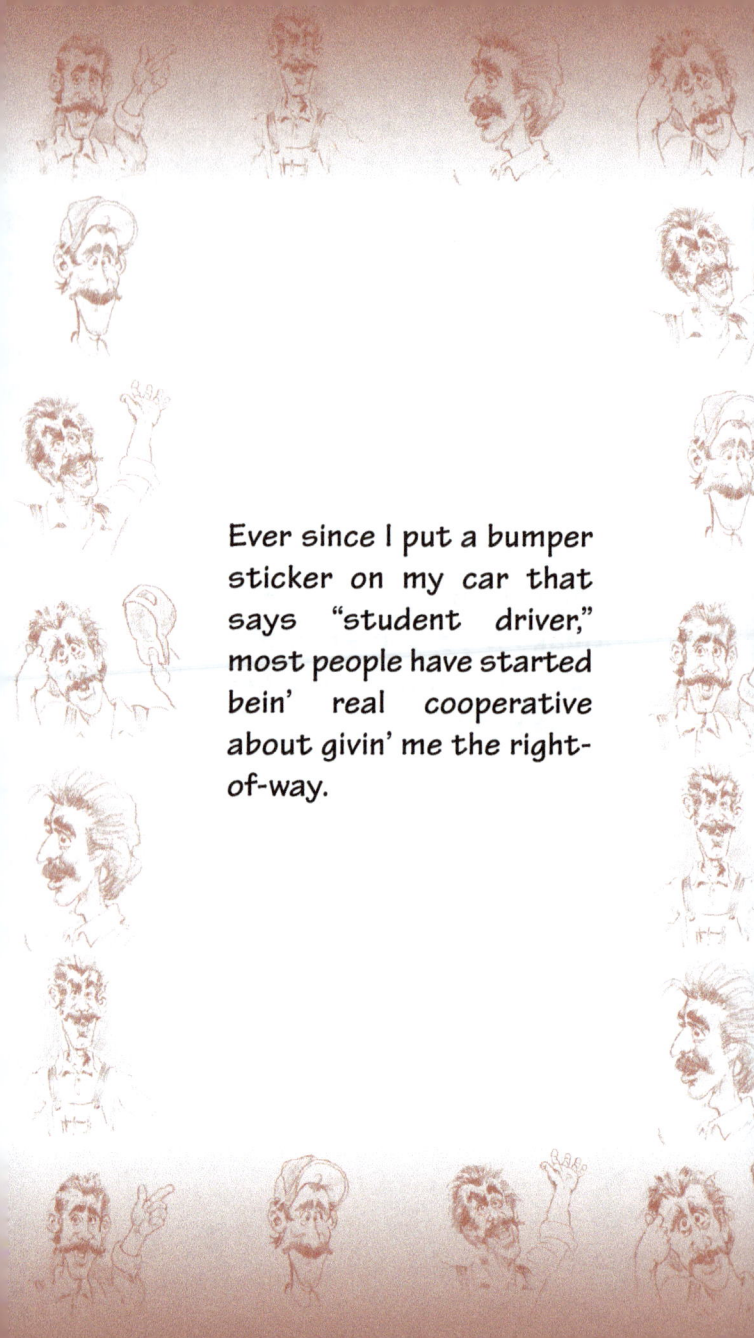

Ever since I put a bumper sticker on my car that says "student driver," most people have started bein' real cooperative about givin' me the right-of-way.

Just because somebody spouts off a lot don't make him a fount of wisdom.

Cell phones are kinda like indecent exposure. A lot of folks talk way too loud about stuff I don't want to hear. There's some things I'd just as soon not know about other people.

I don't spend my time thinkin' about my weaknesses. I don't have to. They just show up by themselves every day.

If you're filthy rich, you probably have much more money than you deserve and more friends than you want. If you're poor as a church mouse, you have far less of both.

Don't go changin' your mind all the time. The one you got is probably bad enough.

I've had my fill of stuck-up people. I've decided, by gum, that I'm never going to speak to any of those people ever again.

Lookin' back on my life, it's actually been pretty boring. I didn't go to my senior prom, I didn't sow any wild oats, I missed my midlife crisis, and now I'm retired and too old to do much of anything. The worst part of it is that I don't care.

I'm for certain that there are multi-millionaires and movie stars who would want to be as content as I am. I chalk it up to just livin' with gratitude.

If you have three apples
and somebody takes away
two of 'em, you've likely
got the bad apple.

The more I read, the more I realize just how ignorant I am, which is why I'm giving up readin' altogether.

Every mornin' when I get up and look in the mirror, I get a harsh dose of reality. That's no way to start a day, so I'm gonna take all the mirrors out of our house.

Sometimes I think I'd give my right arm to be as rich as Donald Trump. But then I'd probably give back all the billions to get my arm back.

If I had lived during the '20s and had the money I have now, I'd probably own the county and that'd be good. Of course, I'd probably be dead by now and that'd be bad.

It downright blows my mind when I hear what professional ball players make these days. Just think what they'd make if they worked all year 'round.

They say that sufferin' is a good teacher. On the other hand, we all need time off from school.

As a part of that vanishin' middle class we hear so much about, I've come to realize that I don't like the rich or the poor. The rich got what I want and the poor want what I got.

People who try to relive
the past probably missed
it the first time around.

The funeral director wanted to sell me a pre-paid funeral package and I told him no thanks. I said I want to be sure that I'm a satisfied customer before I pay him a cent.

I've waited all my life to get old, and now that I'm here I want to enjoy it awhile.

Most folks who run other people down are usually just tryin' to bring every-body else down to their own level.

I'm plannin' to change my ways as soon as I get my fill of the old ones.

Retirement is not all it's trumped up to be. But then again, neither is work.

The only thing poverty and greed have in common is greed.

Don't let an insurance salesman through your door or you might end up buying enough insurance to send his grandkids to school.

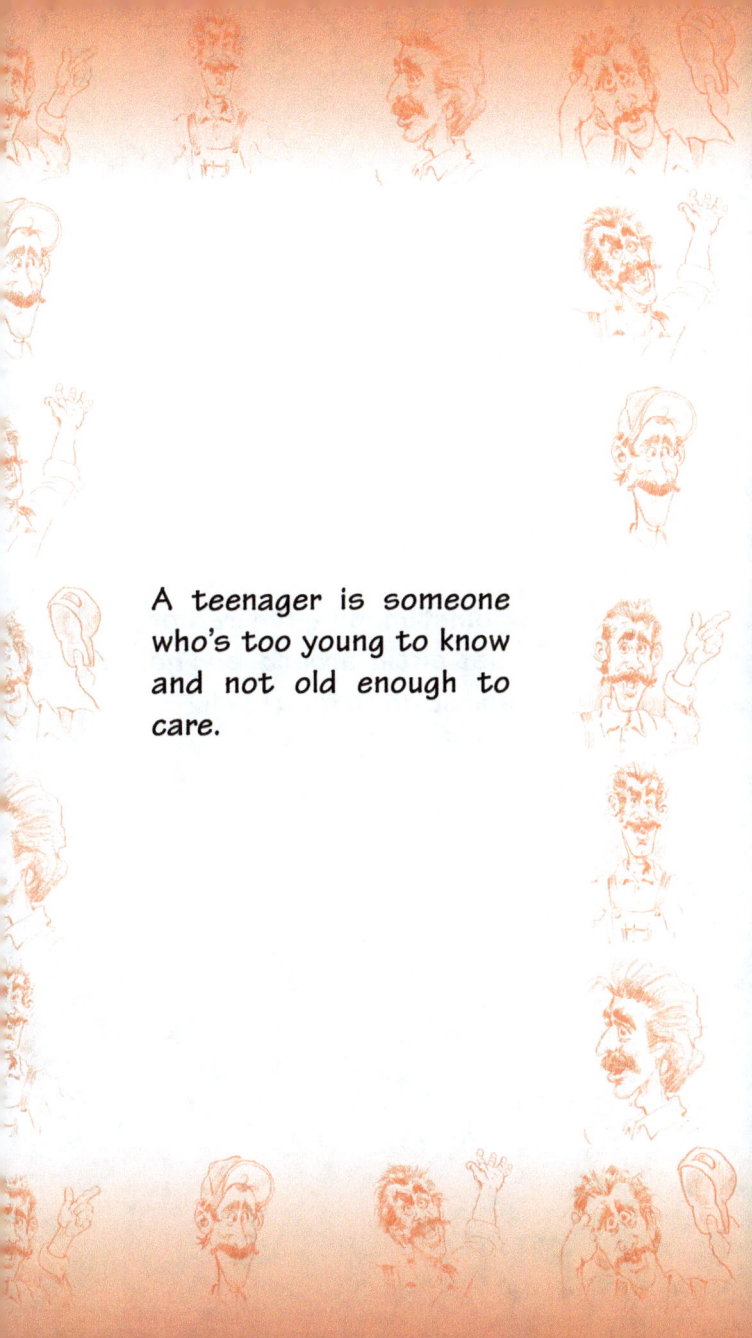

A teenager is someone who's too young to know and not old enough to care.

Sometimes I get tired of just sittin' around, so I go and lie down for a spell.

I loved the good old days when you could leave everything you owned out in the front yard day and night and nobody would steal it. 'Course, in those days we didn't have anything worth stealin'.

A person who thinks he's too old to cry has likely got a big ulcer.

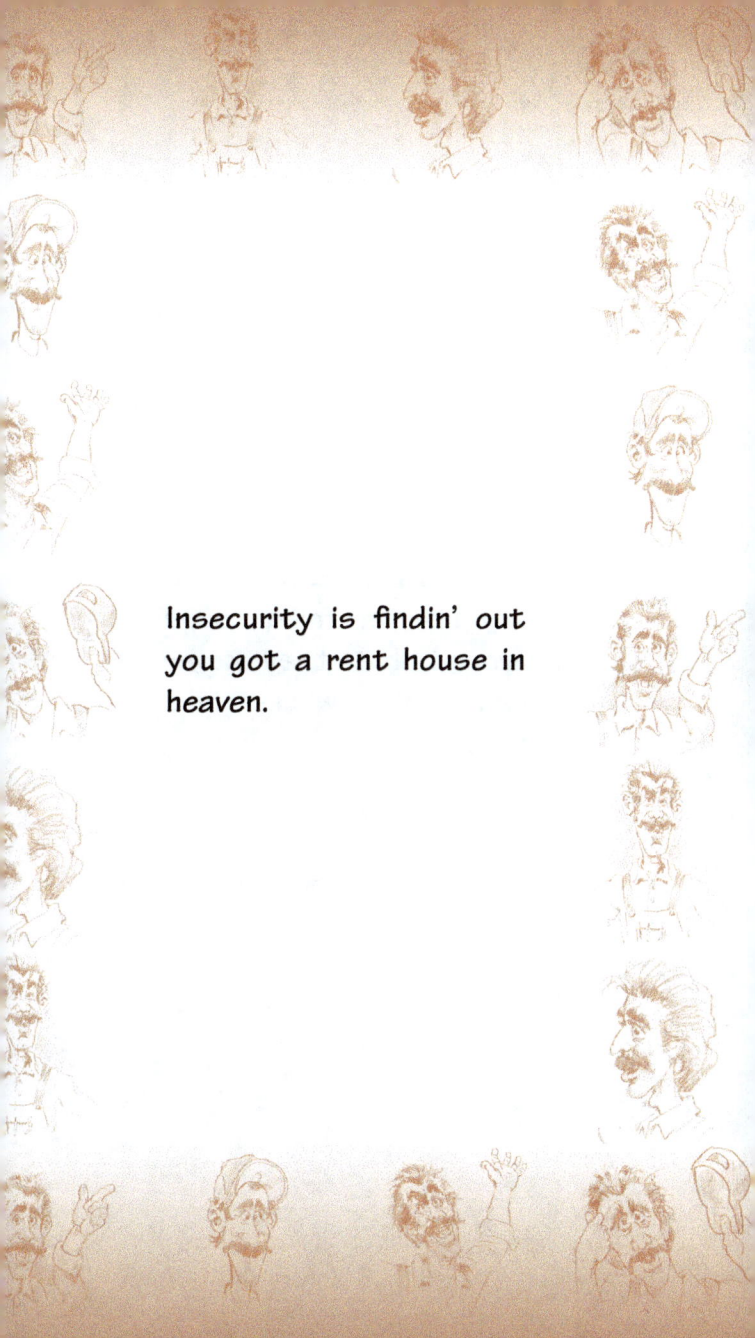

Insecurity is findin' out you got a rent house in heaven.

There are times when I really like for folks to be around, but they never seem to know the right time.

Some people have to be pretty darn smart to cover up all their igno-rance.

I'd give all my money to be ten years younger. Ten dollars for ten years ain't a bad deal.

It's true that the older you get the more you forget, unless you're the IRS. No matter how old they get, they don't forget anything or anybody.

Most folks don't want to hear about your problems, and you don't want to hear about theirs either 'cause you might be one of their problems.

It's true that if you can't say something nice about somebody, you shouldn't say anything at all. So I don't ever say anything about anybody.

If ignorance is bliss, I'm one of the happiest people I know.

When I was 18, I thought I knew everything. Imagine a kid that age thinkin' such a thing when it actually took another 10 years before I could make that claim honestly.

Speakin' of modesty, I'm probably the most humble person I know.

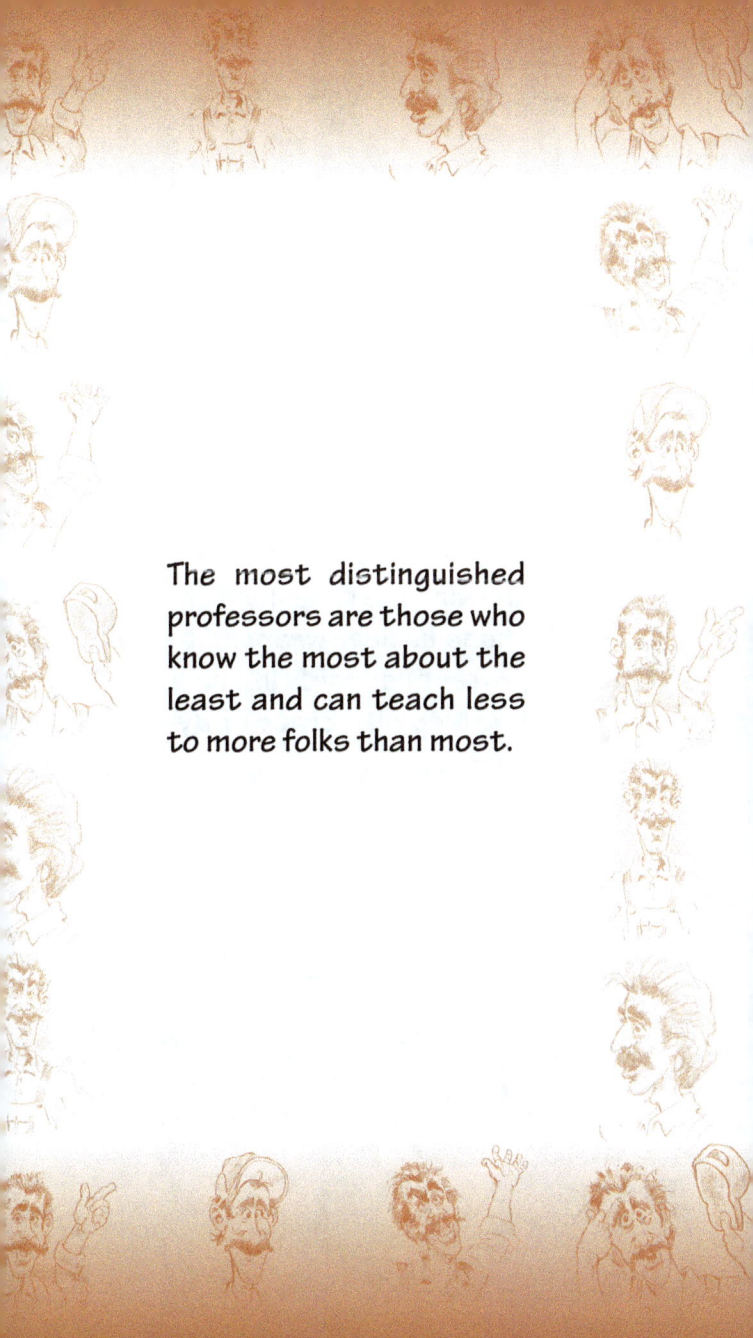

The most distinguished professors are those who know the most about the least and can teach less to more folks than most.

I feel so secure goin' to bed knowin' that we have all those nuclear weapons to protect us. Sorta like goin' to sleep on a crate of dynamite.

Women never look as good in real life as those magazine ads make 'em look. Why, it takes up to three days to put those gals together. After they go through that kind of fuss, you probably couldn't stand to live with 'em.

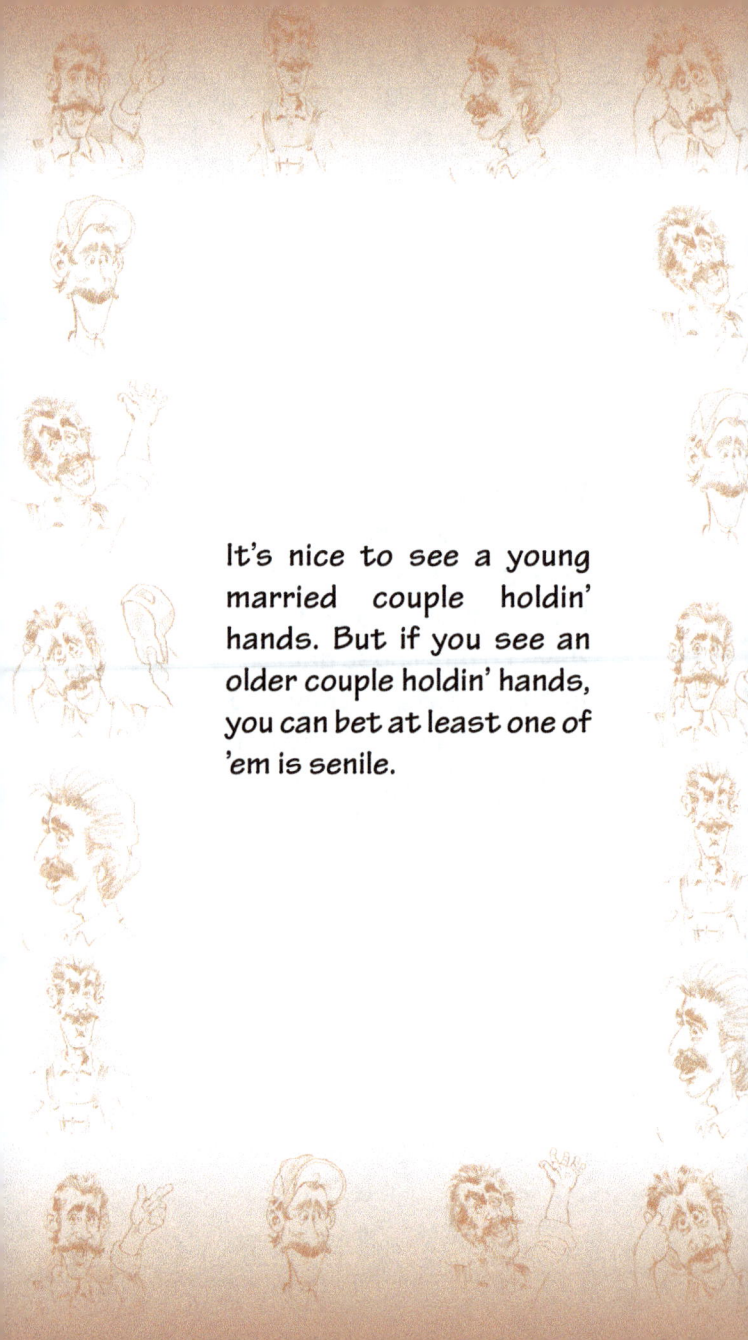

It's nice to see a young married couple holdin' hands. But if you see an older couple holdin' hands, you can bet at least one of 'em is senile.

I ain't seen a middle-class person since sometime before 1980.

What they're payin' as minimum wage these days will just keep a person min-imally alive.

I've never met a man I wouldn't fight. 'Course, I don't get out much.

Riches don't necessarily make a person happy, but neither does poverty.

Someone asked me what I wanted written on my tombstone. I said, *Here lies an empty coffin.*

Did you ever see one of those perpetual care cemeteries? Well, the fact that someone's in there means that is a lie.

You ever notice that the people who talk the most have the least to say?

Love is blind, but hate can find you anywhere.

A person with a quick tem-
per is probably just one
good whippin' short in life.

If a person spends more than ten minutes on the phone, you can likely bet that it was a one-sided conversation.

The other night I dreamed I was in the ring with Rocky Marciano. Luckily, I was saved by the bell. My alarm clock woke me up before the first round.

I never take a nap unless I really feel the need — which is about twice a day, seven days a week.

It's important to remember the past, but it's more important to know how to interpret it.

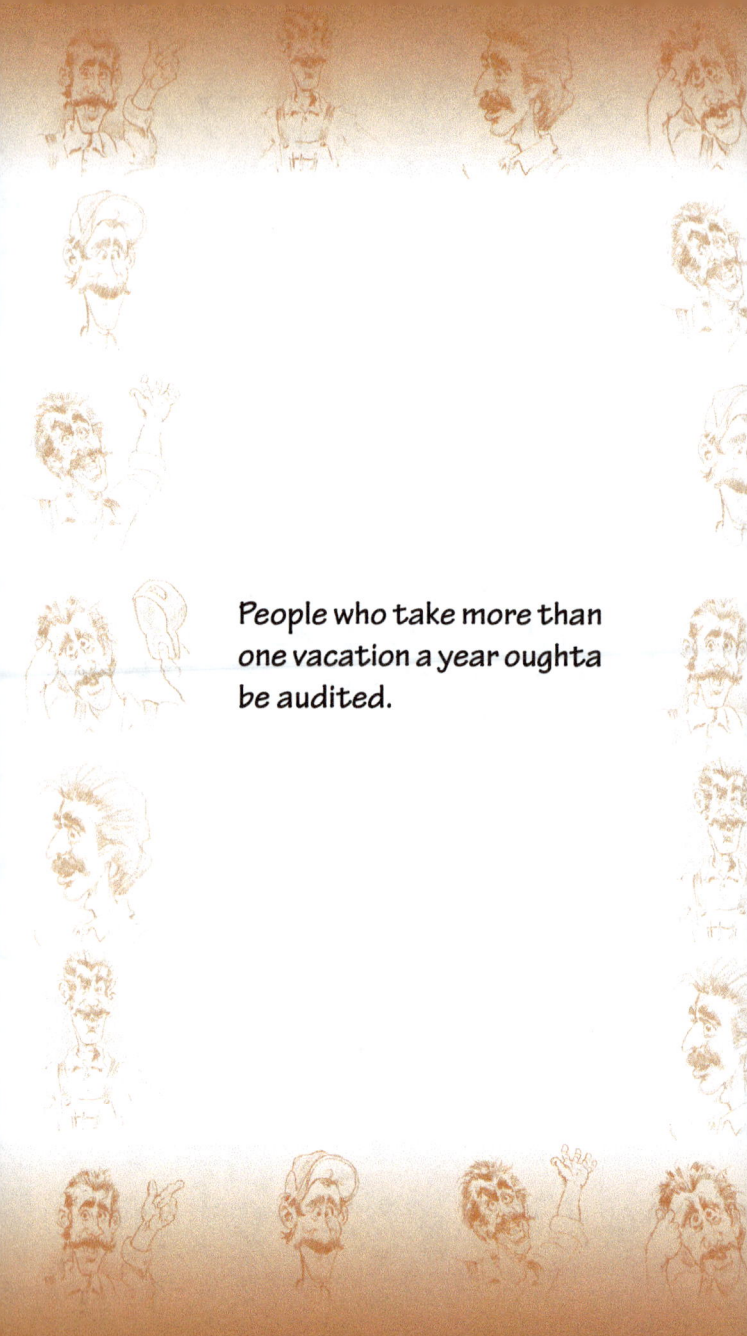

People who take more than
one vacation a year oughta
be audited.

Now that I'm retired, I have more time for what I want to do. Problem is, I spend half the day restin' from the day before and the other half restin' up for the next day.

After plantin' my garden in early spring, I realized that I don't care for spendin' so many hours a day keepin' the weeds out. It's a waste of precious time when you realize that one day all you'll be doin' is pushin' up daisies.

Health 'n' Such

I don't think those drug companies should be allowed to advertise on TV. In the first place, nobody can get a drug without a doctor's say so. In the second place, who in their right mind wouldn't be scared to take one of the drugs after hearin' about all the side effects? In the third place, spendin' all that money on advertisements makes the drugs a lot more expensive for the folks whose doctors say they have to take 'em.

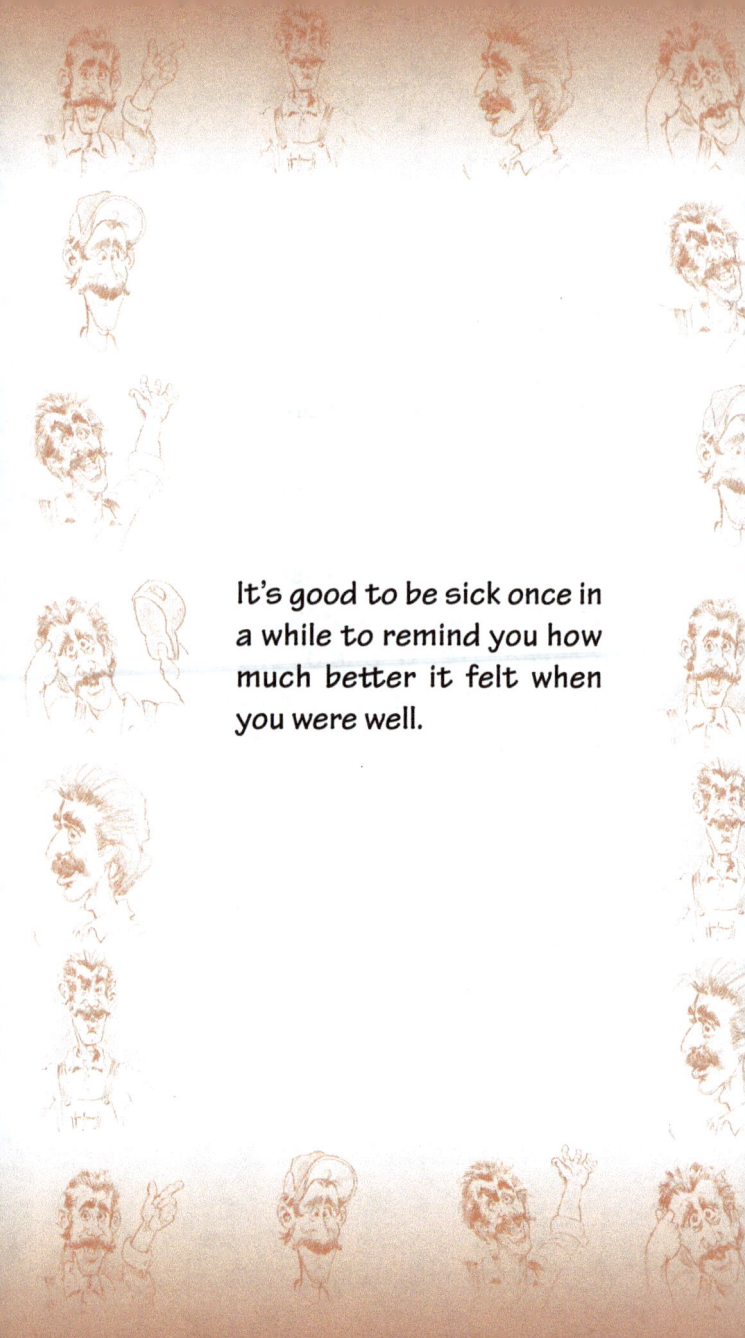

It's good to be sick once in a while to remind you how much better it felt when you were well.

My doctor told me I oughta slow down a bit on my work around the farm. I told him I could slow down on my work if he'd lower his fees.

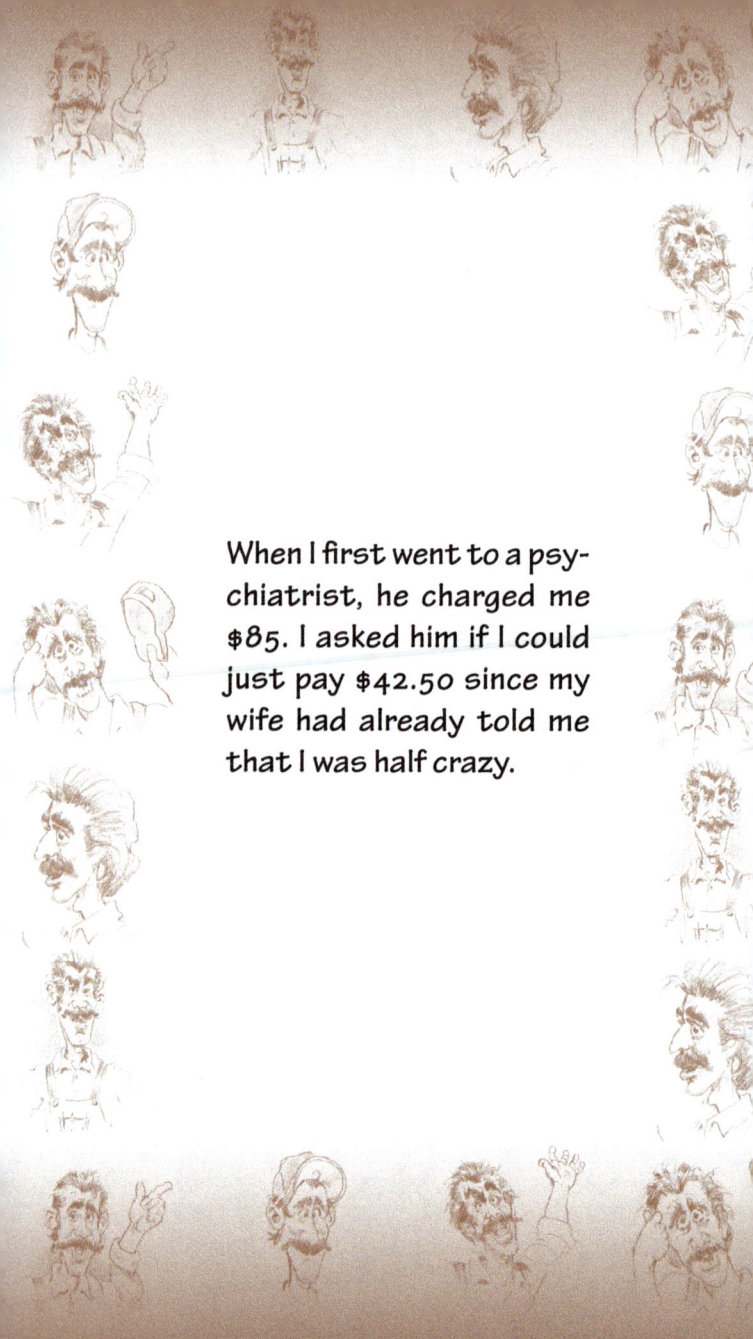

When I first went to a psychiatrist, he charged me $85. I asked him if I could just pay $42.50 since my wife had already told me that I was half crazy.

I didn't know I had so many problems until I went to the psychiatrist. After a year of counselin', I think it's helped the psychiatrist more than it's helped me. I may be somewhat saner, but he's darned sure a whole lot richer.

I told my doctor that since he had taken out my appendix, gall bladder, tonsils and adenoids, I oughta be gettin' at least a 20% discount 'cause there was that much less of me to take care of.

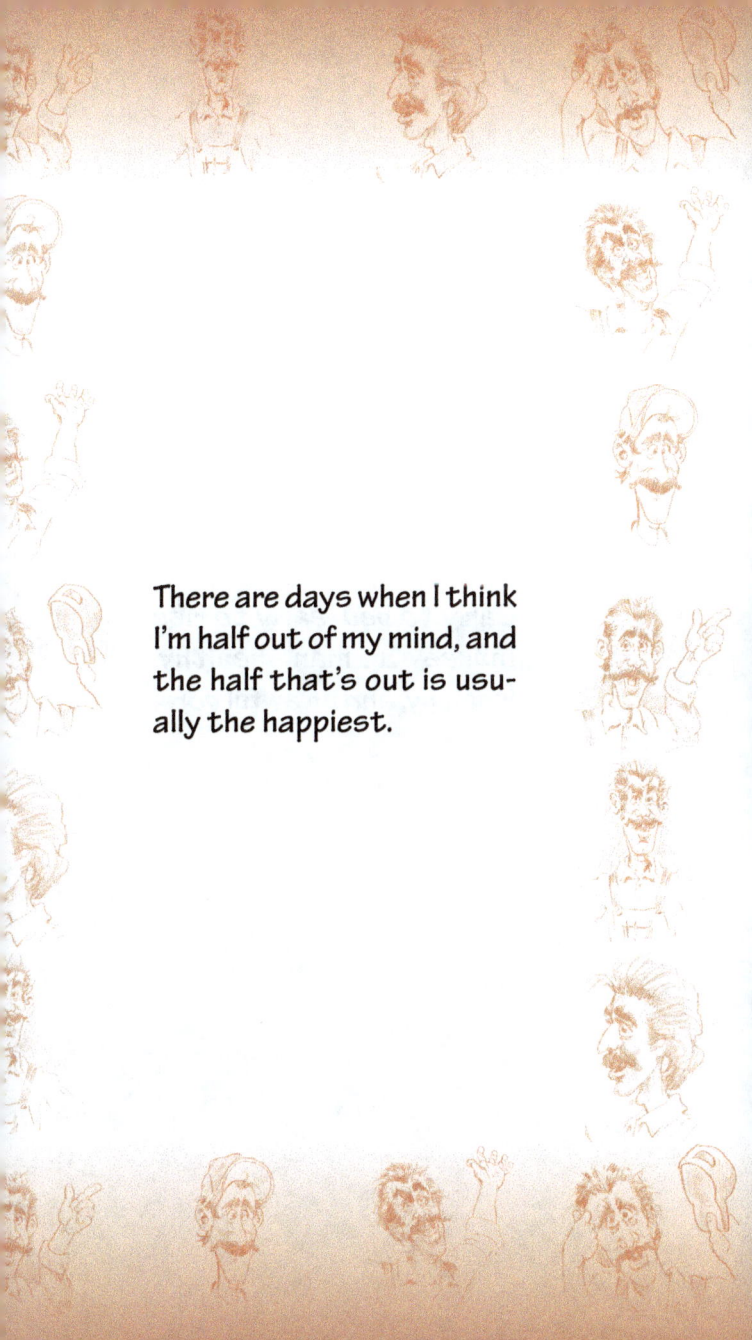

There are days when I think
I'm half out of my mind, and
the half that's out is usually the happiest.

Early to bed, early to rise makes a man healthy, wealthy, and an awful bore.

My doctor told me that with an operation I would have a 50/50 chance of livin' to a ripe old age. I told him I'd wait till the odds are better.

There's no use worryin' about death. It'll come sooner or later.

Whoever said that the way to a man's heart is through his stomach is not the person you'd want to do your bypass surgery.

A few years ago my wife and I started havin' big problems. We finally broke down and went to see one of those therapists. At the end of our visit he said, *The way I figure it, you two are lucky and you've also done some other folks a big favor. You are probably the only two people that could live with either one of you, and you saved two other people a whole bunch of heartache.*

I don't much care for my podiatrist. A person has to stoop pretty low to do that kind of work.

Did you hear about the hematologist who shared office space with a gastroenterologist? Their practice was called *Blood and Guts*.

We have this hematologist in town whose name is Dr. Dracula. He says he likes what he does because it's the kind of work he can get his teeth into. He sure is one of the most vein men I've ever known.

I went to the doctor the other day and the nurse asked me what kind of drugs I was taking. I said, *What kind of drugs are you offerin'?*

Our local neurologist recently quit her work. I heard she was sufferin' anxiety attacks, so I guess you could say she'd lost her nerve.

I had to change chiropractors last month. The last one I went to rubbed me the wrong way.

I know two proctologists. One's an optimist and the other's a pessimist. The optimist's motto is *All's well that ends well.* The pessimist's motto is *The end is near.*

My doctor put me on a 1,200-calorie diet. I manage to stay full, though, 'cause I'm now takin' lots of antidepressants.

Lately I've been goin' to bed real early and gettin' up real late. My psychiatrist told me that's a sign that I'm likely sufferin' from depression. I think it's a sign that I'm just gettin' lazy.

Last time I went to the doctor, he put me on a treadmill for 15 minutes. After that he asked me how I felt. I said the treadmill was a lot like life — a lot of work, and you don't get anywhere.

The doctor asked me if I had any complaints when I went in for a checkup. I told him that food and gas prices are too high, and taxes are darned near takin' everything else I've got.

Did you hear about the doctor who went mad? He lost all his patients.

My doctor told me that I need to quit eatin' snacks between meals, so now I'm eatin' 'em with my meals.

They say that age is a state of mind. That's what worries me.

I may be old, but I'm also slow.

When I was in the hospital for surgery last year, a nurse came into my room and said she was gonna give me a bath. I asked her if she thought she could fly to the moon. She said, *Why, no!* I told her it was more likely she would fly to the moon than give me a bath.

Religion 'n' Politics

I've always dreamed of being President. Then I wake up to the reality that the cows need to be milked.

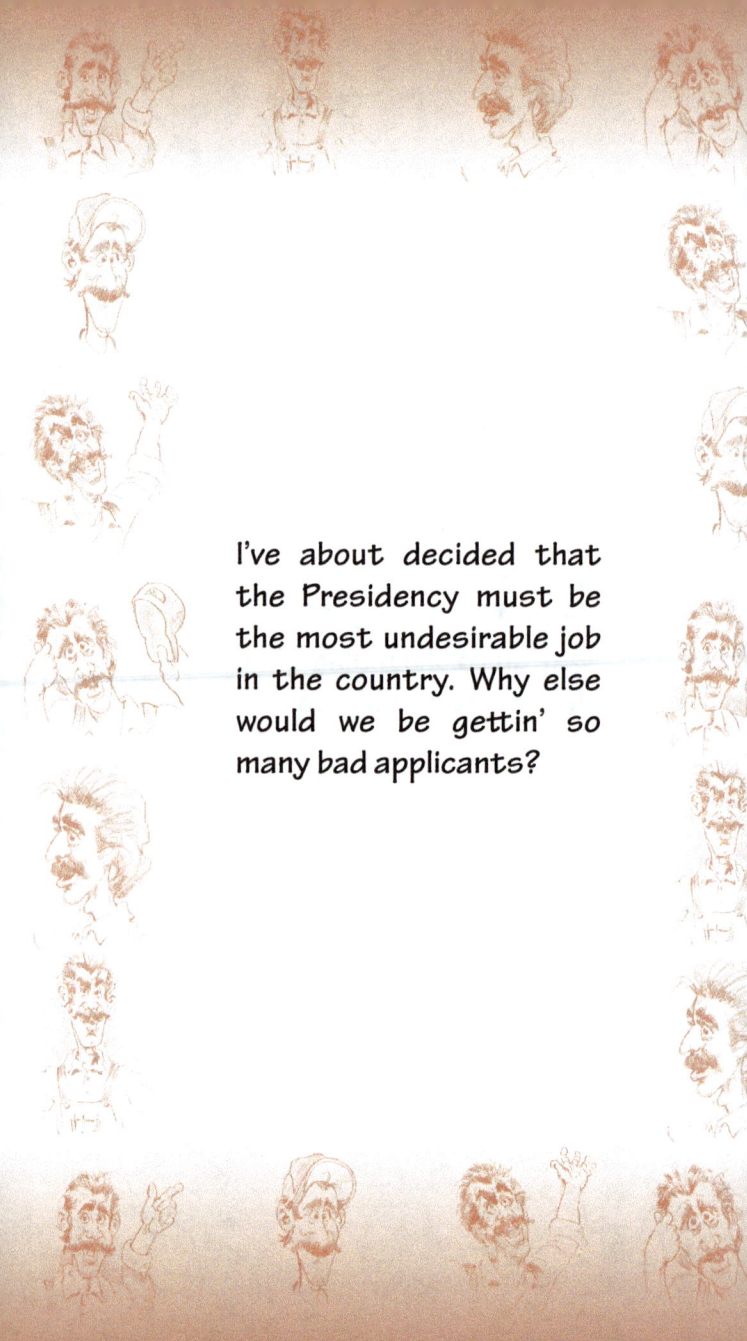

I've about decided that the Presidency must be the most undesirable job in the country. Why else would we be gettin' so many bad applicants?

You have to be at least 35 years old to be President, and you have to be dead 100 years to have been a great one.

A lot of folks say God helps those who help themselves. Well, there's a bunch of greedy people out there who are helpin' themselves to much more than they need, and I don't believe God has anything to do with it.

You gotta hand it to politi-cians. They're smart enough to promise us the moon, but then they often deliver somethin' less lofty—hell on earth.

The almighty dollar is not only *runnin'* our country. In many ways, it's *ruinin'* our country.

I think before this nation
ever goes to war, it oughta
be put up for a vote from
everybody in the country.
And those who vote to go
to war oughta be the first
ones sent to fight.

It's bein' a hypocrite if you say you love and admire Jesus but you neglect the lessons from his words and his lifestyle.

There used to be a difference between Democrats and Republicans, but there's not that much difference anymore. Most all of our politicians are owned lock, stock, and barrel by the fat-cat banks and corporations.

A nation oughta be ashamed of braggin' about the number of billionaires it has when more than twenty per cent of its children don't get enough to eat.

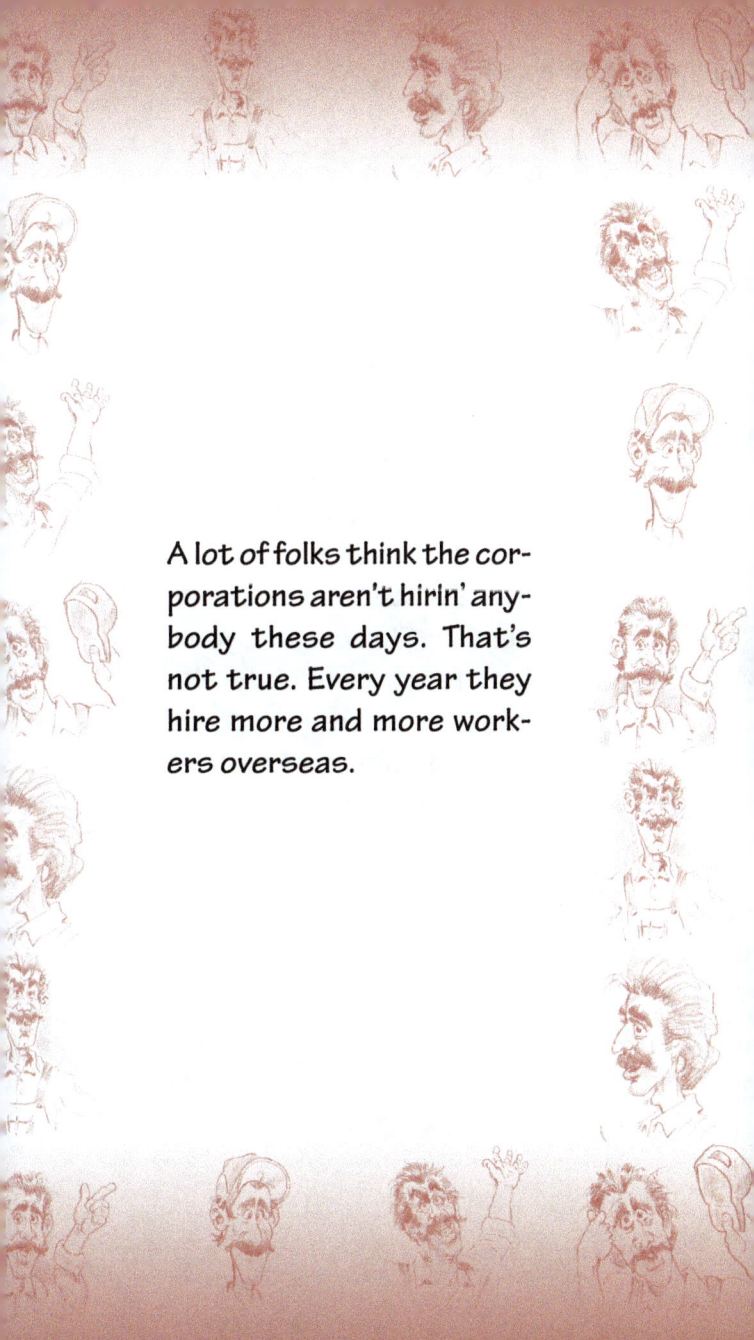

A lot of folks think the corporations aren't hirin' anybody these days. That's not true. Every year they hire more and more workers overseas.

Speakin' of overseas workers, it's gettin' so a body
might as well not bother
callin' a customer service
number. Chances are, you'll
just reach somebody who
has such a strange accent
that you can't make heads
or tails of what they're
sayin'.

Whoever started callin' climate change Global Warmin' made a big mistake, 'cause there are a lot of folks who believe climate change is a hoax since it gets cold in the winter. Anybody who is payin' attention to the new weather patterns around the world oughta be able to get the picture that there's a heap of strange stuff goin' on with our climate.

This TV preacher said he wanted folks to send him $50 for a prayer cloth. I sent him my prayer cloth and a bill for $50.

A simple economic principle is that there's not ever enough to go around, which means that a few people usually take too much and most people are left with too little.

My sister sent money to one of those TV preachers who said that money sent to him was plantin' seeds for prosperity. He forgot to mention that it was his own prosperity he was talkin' about. Next thing we knew, that preacher had bought himself a jet airplane and my sister still can't pay her rent.

I hear there's a new local chapter of the KKK that has a choir. They use sheet music.

I know a lot of church folks who pray all the time for God to bless their lives. It seems to me that if they can't see the blessings they already have, they wouldn't be able to appreciate any new ones.

There's a bunch of Baptists who are always rantin' about other people's drinkin', dancin', and gamblin'. Like as not, they're mad 'cause other folks are havin' a better time than they are.

I've never seen a pious person who was half as good as he thought he was, and I've never seen a sinner who was half as bad as he thought he was.

No matter how the economy is doin', integrity always seems to be in short supply.

I was in Dallas a while back and saw where one of those TV preachers who claims to be a healer was havin' a big rally. That got me to thinkin' about folks in the hospitals who were too sick to get out of bed and attend the rally. Seems to me that if God really did call that man to be a healer, He would've wanted him to stop by the hospitals and heal the folks there while he was in town.

A lot of people who claim to be spiritually-minded make idols of themselves.

Preachers and politicians are a lot alike. They want everybody to hang on their every word, and too often we do.

Television preachers turn me off, so I usually do the same to them.

I don't have any problem believin' in scriptures. My problem is with those preachers who try to tell me the scriptures mean somethin' that I know darned well they don't.

It's a good thing the government don't jail the con artists on Wall Street. We'd have to build a whole bunch of new prisons.

Sometimes I hate to go to church 'cause I get woozy from the smell of all of those ladies' perfumes. Must be that the French have invented a new perfume called *Eau de Pew*.

Folks who think of themselves as super-spiritual have probably never raised children.

I'm thinkin' this nation will have true democracy when a minimum-wage worker has as much political clout as those overpaid corporate executives.

It's downright hypocritical to pray in church for the poor and needy and then go out and vote for politicians who make policies that further penalize the poor and needy.

Bufordpedia

Indecent Exposure

Where there's too much ugly showin'.

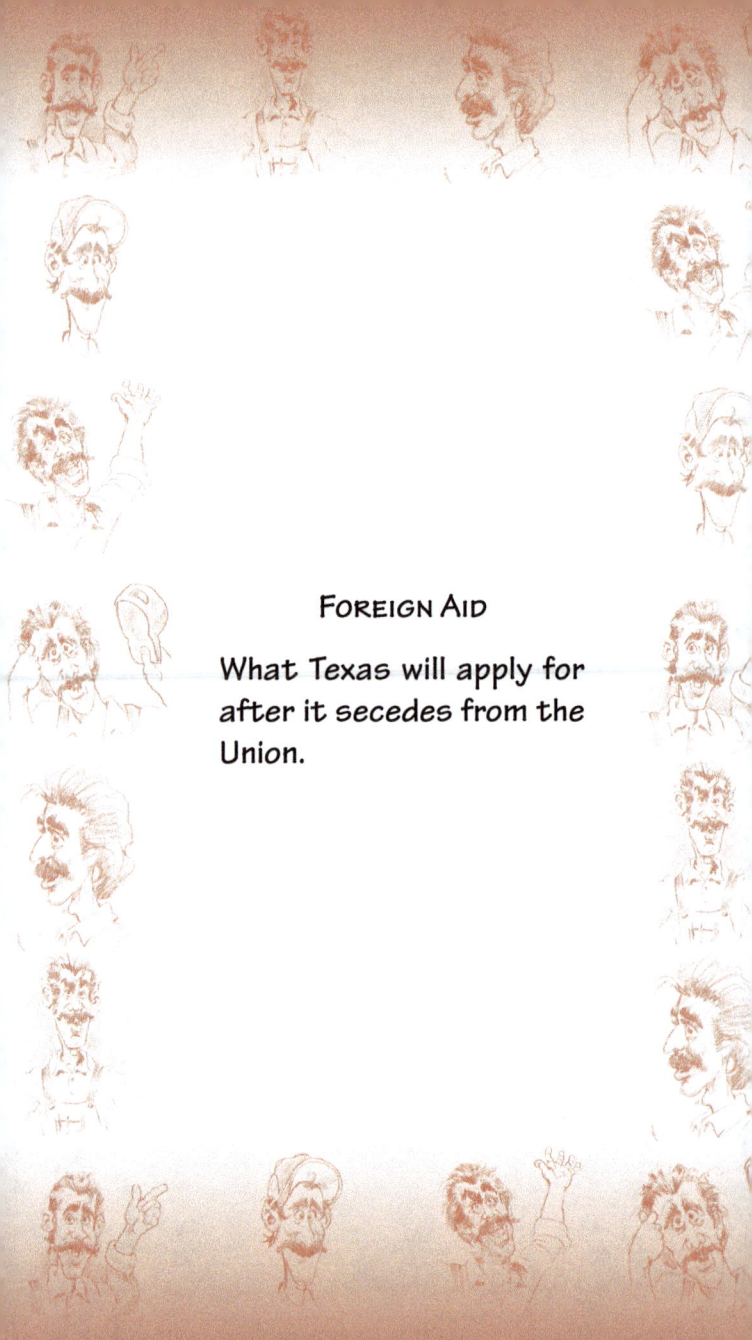

FOREIGN AID

What Texas will apply for after it secedes from the Union.

MIDLIFE CRISIS

When you realize that the only things left that can hold up your pants are your suspenders.

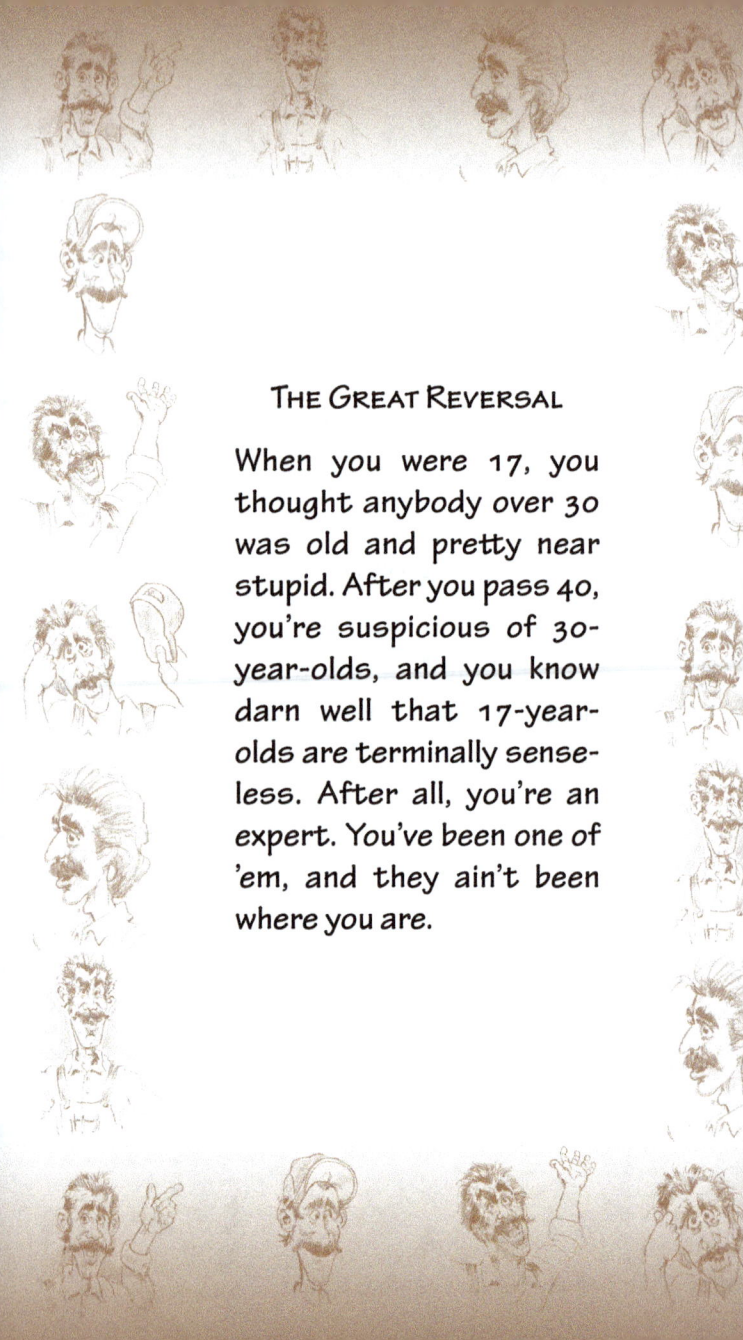

The Great Reversal

When you were 17, you thought anybody over 30 was old and pretty near stupid. After you pass 40, you're suspicious of 30-year-olds, and you know darn well that 17-year-olds are terminally senseless. After all, you're an expert. You've been one of 'em, and they ain't been where you are.

Government Handouts

The largest amount of these are tax breaks for all the fat cats and corporations . . . not what the poor welfare mothers, who need help from the government to feed their families, receive.

Hell

Where every tyrant, murderer, thief, rapist, and abusive husband is given a conscience and then forced to live with it for eternity.

Preparation for Death

The final meal the night before you take off for the Sweet By-and-By. You get your favorite dish of fried chicken, garlic mashed potatoes, fried okra, corn on the cob, biscuits with gravy, and cherry cobbler with homemade vanilla ice cream. 'Course, if you weren't really scheduled for departure, this meal could make that happen.

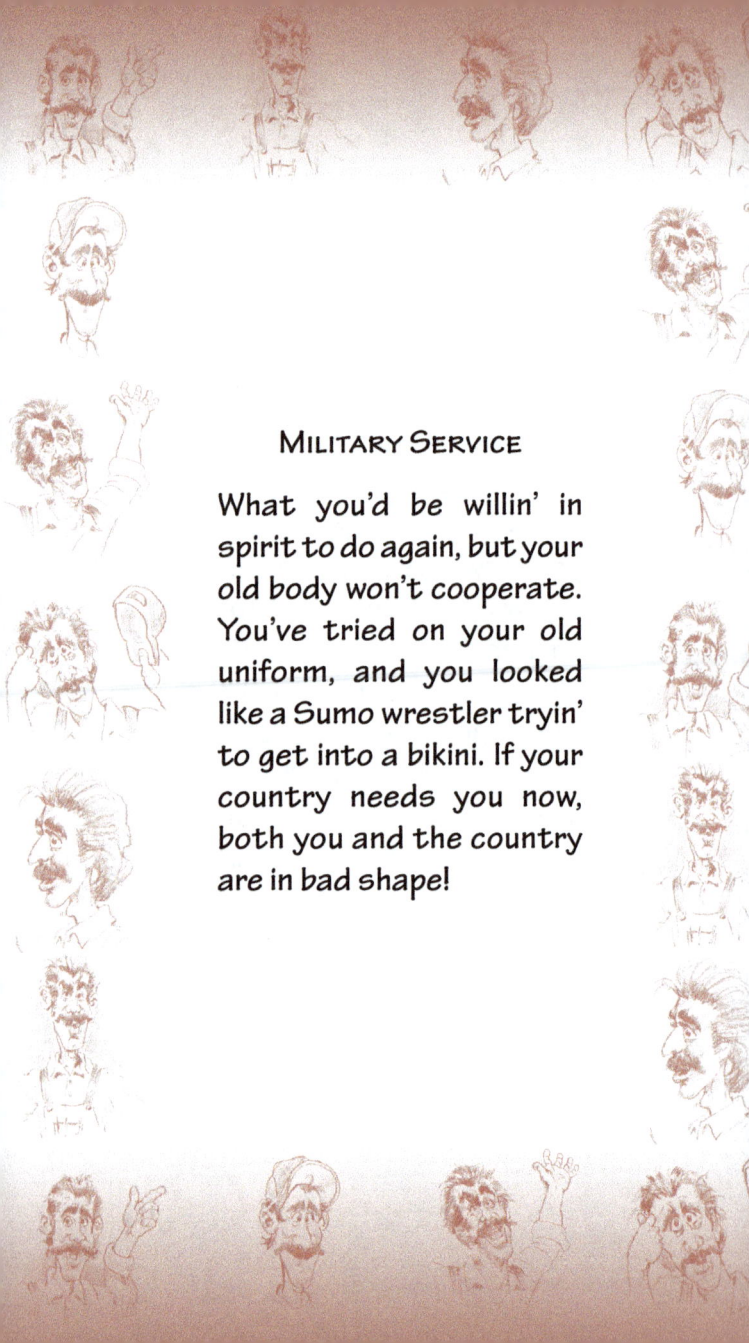

MILITARY SERVICE

What you'd be willin' in spirit to do again, but your old body won't cooperate. You've tried on your old uniform, and you looked like a Sumo wrestler tryin' to get into a bikini. If your country needs you now, both you and the country are in bad shape!

Big-Time Preachers

Ministers who drive big, fancy cars and live on an estate. Smart people don't like to give money to churches or evangelistic associations led by those ministers, 'cause that seems like the middleman is takin' too much of a cut.

BIG CITY FOLK

People who you hope will stay in their cities. You hear that a ton of 'em are thinkin' about movin' to your little town, so you ask the local Chamber of Commerce to tell prospective newcomers that we have the highest crime rate per capita of any city in the U.S., that we've had fourteen fatalities this year at our one and only stoplight, that the town drunk is a former member of the Charles Manson gang, and that both the Crips and Bloods have members here.

Rush Limbaugh

A bag of wind. We can keep prayin' that he'll be kicked off the air or run out of air.

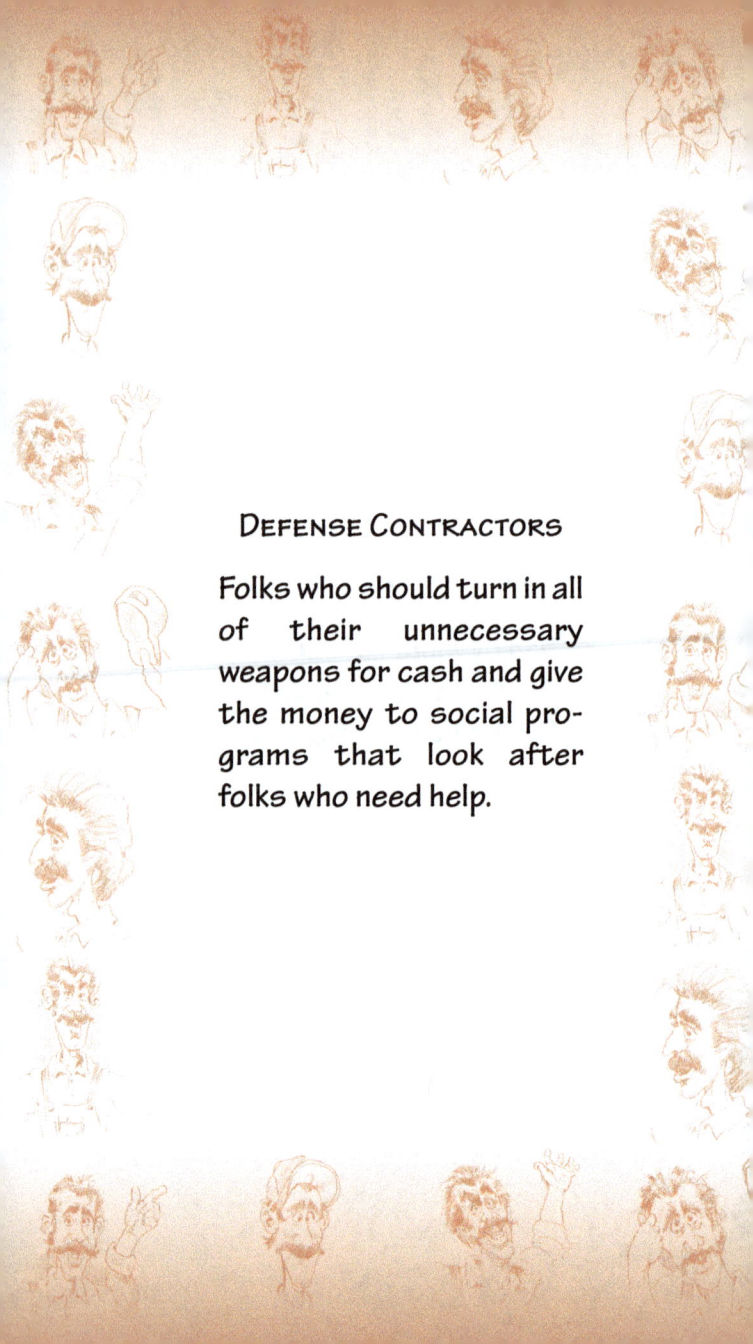

Defense Contractors

Folks who should turn in all of their unnecessary weapons for cash and give the money to social pro-grams that look after folks who need help.

REALITY CHECK

The one I write to the IRS once a year.

GUT CHECK

When you eat ranch-style beans with jalapenos, onions, and hot sauce.

Blank Check

What's left after you pay
all of your bills.

PERFECT MARRIAGE

(See DELUSIONS)

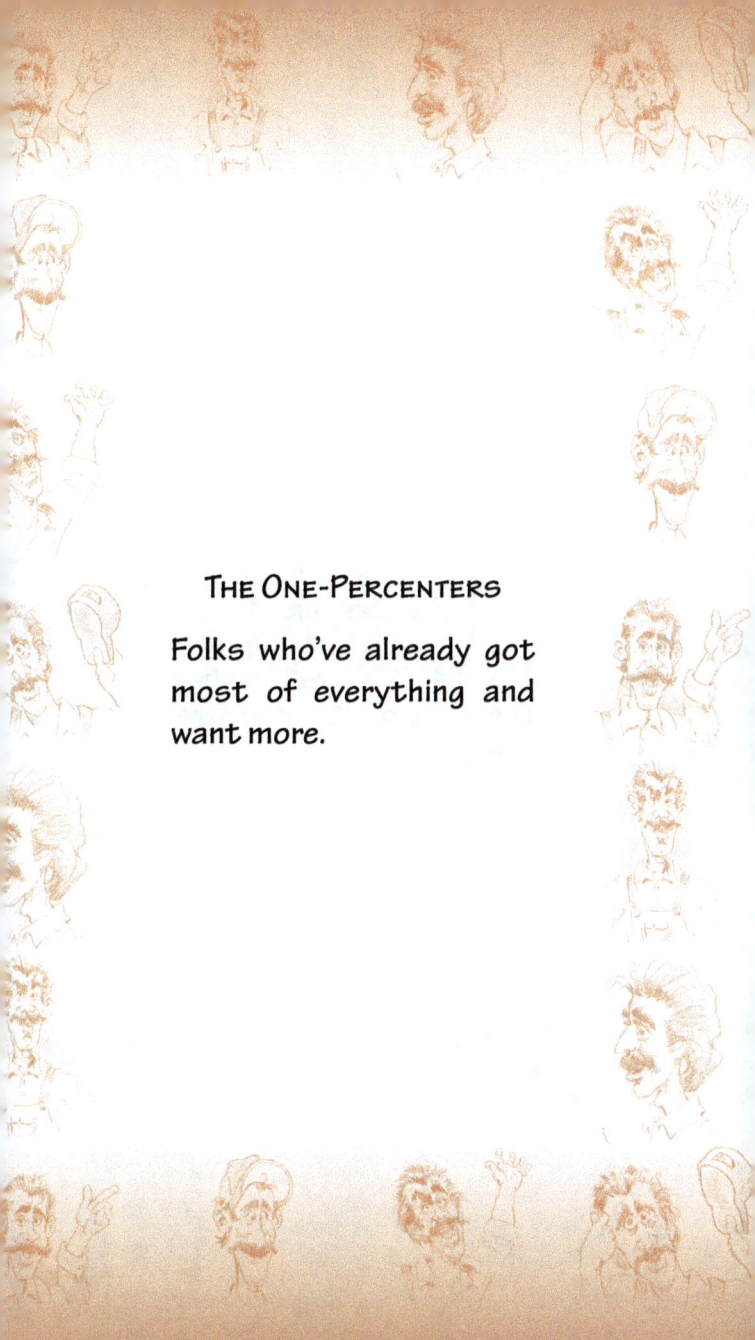

The One-Percenters

Folks who've already got most of everything and want more.

THE NINETY-NINE PERCENTERS

The ones who might launch the second American Revolution.

Free Trade Agreement

What was ever "free" about it?

Government Surveillance

Santa really is watchin' to see whether you're naughty or nice.

DEMOCRACY

Our government that's been replaced by Corporatocracy.

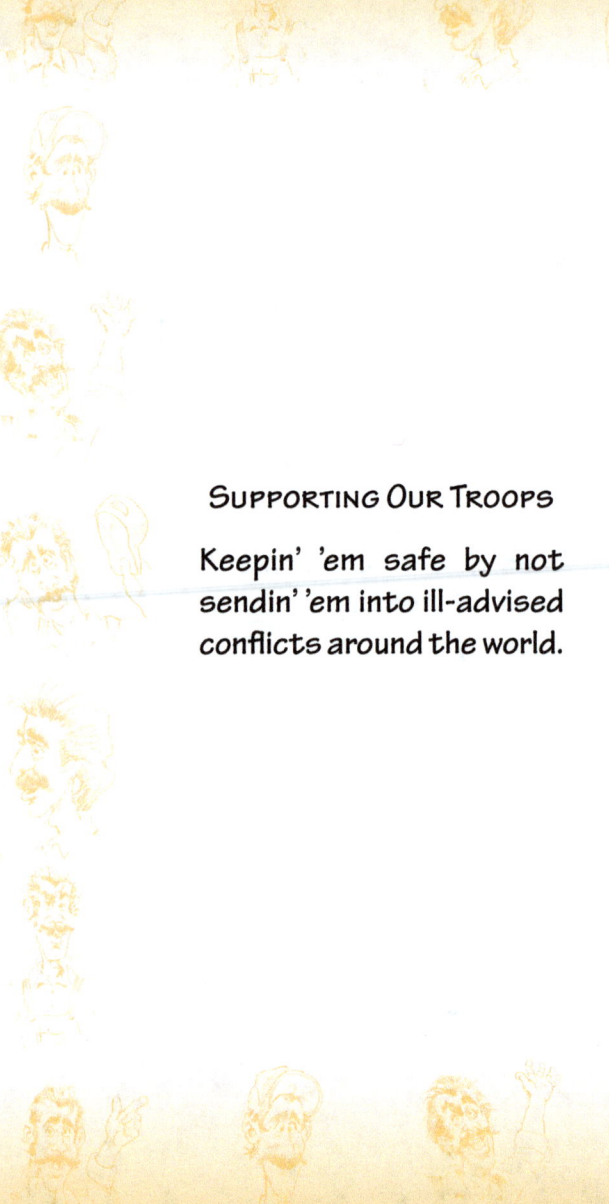

Supporting Our Troops

Keepin' 'em safe by not sendin' 'em into ill-advised conflicts around the world.

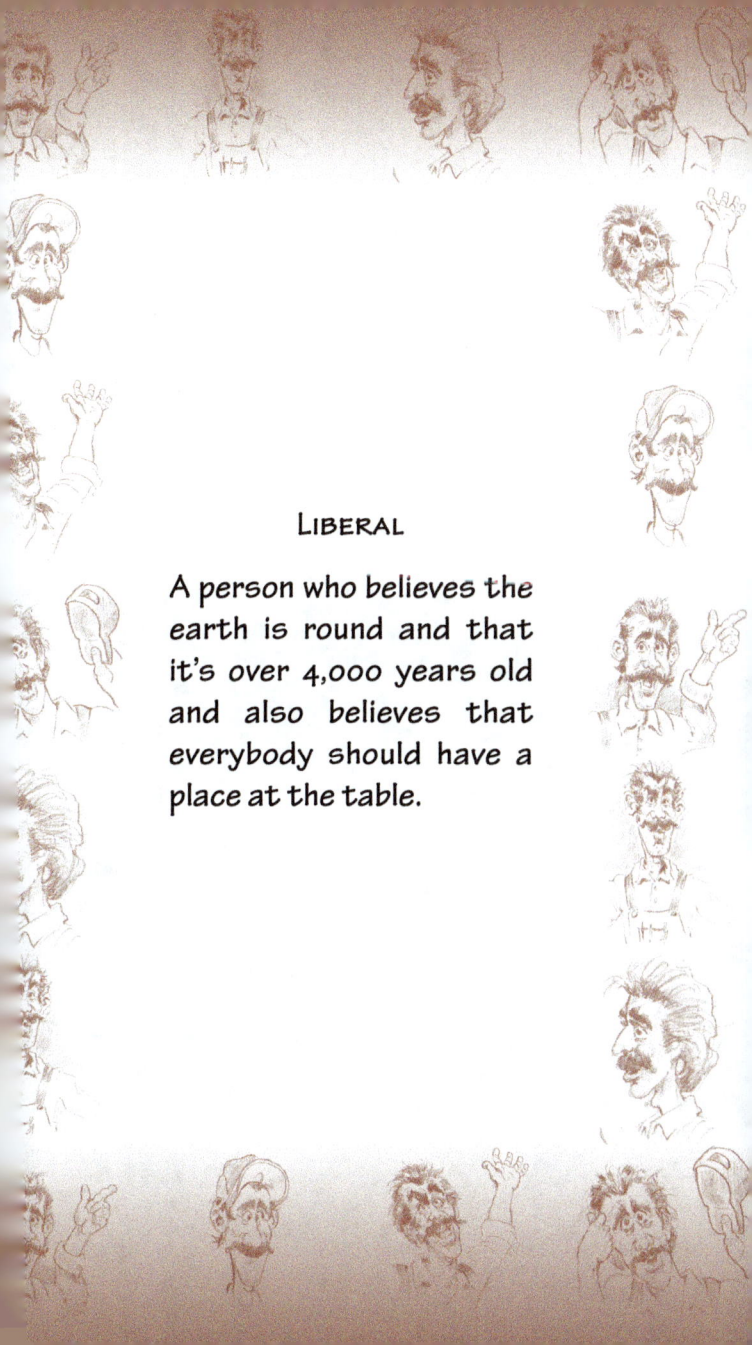

Liberal

A person who believes the earth is round and that it's over 4,000 years old and also believes that everybody should have a place at the table.